TERMINAL DIALOG

"Good morning, Missile 1848," he said. His words floated up on the display screen as the terminal converted speech to print. "Have your modifications been completed?"

"Yes, Commander," appeared on the screen. "The GMB Mark II has been replaced with a GMB Mark IC4, configured for maximum range. It is installed and properly seated."

"Very good, 1848. I am now going to give you the terminal ballistic description to go with the course information you already have. Are you ready to receive?"

"Affirmative," was the missile's laconic reply.

The officer keyed in the Security computer, which transferred the file on Mundito Rosinante.

"Thank you for target information," floated up on the screen. "Is present warhead satisfactory?"

"What is the yield of your present warhead?"

"Nominal yield of warhead #41287.42 is one megaton. The warhead, however, is 9 years, 4 months old and will probably yield no more than 96 percent nominal value with normal detonation protocol."

"That appears satisfactory," the man said. "Maintain readiness to launch for twenty-four hours."

"This missile is gratified to be of use."

Long Shot
for Rosinante

Alexis A. Gilliland

A Del Rey Book

BALLANTINE BOOKS • NEW YORK

A Del Rey Book
Published by Ballantine Books

Library of Congress, Catalog Card Number: 81-66664

ISBN 0-345-29854-3

Manufactured in the United States of America

First edition: October 1981

Cover art by Rick Sternbach

Illustrations by Chris Barbieri

This book is dedicated
to Charles, who has
started to clean up his room.

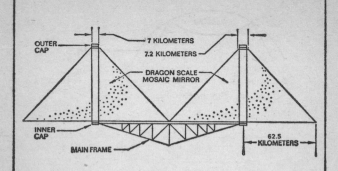

FIGURE 1: a. Mundito Rosinante assembly

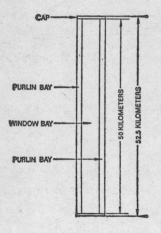

b. Vertical cross-section of a rotating cylinder

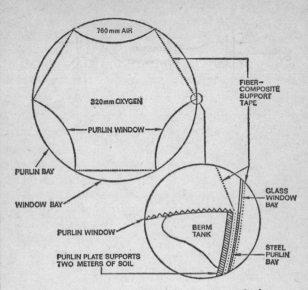

FIGURE 2: Sun-end view of a rotating cylinder

760 mm AIR

320mm OXYGEN

PURLIN WINDOW

PURLIN BAY

WINDOW BAY

FIBER–COMPOSITE SUPPORT TAPE

GLASS WINDOW BAY

PURLIN WINDOW

BERM TANK

PURLIN PLATE SUPPORTS TWO METERS OF SOIL

STEEL PURLIN BAY

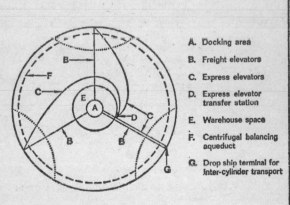

A. Docking area

B. Freight elevators

C. Express elevators

D. Express elevator transfer station

E. Warehouse space

F. Centrifugal balancing aqueduct

G. Drop ship terminal for inter-cylinder transport

FIGURE 3: End view of outer cap

CHAPTER 1

William Marvin Hulvey removed his black raincoat and handed it to the serving robot, which gave him a green plastic check.

"Okay, Stan," he said, "the President wants to see me. I don't suppose you'd have any inkling or suspicion why, would you?"

Stanley Bowman, the Administrator of NAUGA-Security, smiled faintly and polished his rimless glasses with an immaculate handkerchief.

"I didn't say he wanted to see you, Willy, I said he *needed* to see you. He probably can't attach your name to your face, but believe me, Willy, President Forbes is in need of your services."

"Look, Stan, if the man needs my services, all he has to do is write me a memorandum. Right? Of course right."

An impeccably tailored Secret Service man walked up and led them into the atrium of the Presidential Mansion, where a tall, balding man was standing under the pink-and-white flowering dogwoods with a glass of bourbon in his hand.

"Bob," said Stanley Bowman, "this is William Hulvey, my Commissioner of the Military Intelligence Service. Willy, this is Robert Schlecter, the President's Appointments Secretary."

They shook hands.

"Can I get you something to drink?" asked Schlecter.

"No," said Hulvey. "I drink, but not now."

"I expect you're right," said Schlecter, "but it's been a bad day."

President John R. Forbes walked in.

"Do you know Mr. Hulvey, sir?" asked Bowman.

"We've met," said the President. "Bob, put down that goddamn drink and play the videotape. I expect they may have seen it, but it saves talking."

Schlecter put down his drink and turned on the television set.

"In this afternoon's top story," said the announcer, "the Supreme Court has just ruled that *The Star of Mexicali* cannot be enjoined from leaving Laputa for the asteroids. *The Star of Mexicali*, as you may recall, is carrying nearly twenty-five hundred Texican students—all Anglos—arrested at the Alamo riots during Easter vacation. The court declined to comment on the legality of transporting the students from San Antonio to the orbital city of Laputa, saying that the welfare of the ozone layer was not at issue. The court added that Texas Governor Panoblanco clearly did not have any permit for the shuttle flight in question, and that in view of the present condition of the ozone layer one would have probably not been issued."

"How can you listen to the fool?" asked Hulvey. "He keeps rehashing ancient history and serving it up as sirloin steak."

"Hush," said the President.

". . . upheld the lower court ruling on the point that a state of the North American Union retains control of a corvée after it leaves the state until it enters another state. This is being hailed as a stunning victory for the antihegemonists, since until now no limit has been placed on the Federal Government's claim to control the volume of space beyond the—"

Schlecter turned the set off.

"That's it," he said. "We have a bill in the hopper to authorize NAUGA-Navy to intercept *The Star of Mexicali* in space, but the antihegemonists will filibuster, and I figure we lack maybe six or seven votes to invoke cloture."

He picked up his glass and took a drink.

"It isn't that anybody is supporting Governor Panoblanco on this, but the antihegemonists want this one pretty damn bad."

"There's serious talk of secession for the first time in twenty years," said Bowman. "The Governor is rolling around like a loose cannon. Personally, he's a joke, a spick idiot. He isn't serious, but the people waiting to pick up the pieces are something else."

"Will no one rid me of this pestilent Governor?" asked the President.

Bowman turned to Hulvey.

"Couldn't something be arranged, Willy?" he asked mildly.

Hulvey stared at him for a moment.

"Don't be a fool, Stan," he said at last, "a dead skunk smells worse than a live one."

"Now, now, Willy," said Bowman soothingly, "don't take on like that. Some things have just got to be done, and this looks like it might be one of them."

"*The Star of Mexicali*," said Hulvey, "where is it headed?"

"Asteroid Rosinante," replied Schlecter. "Scadiwa has a project up there for the students to staff up."

"One of *those*," said Hulvey. "Seems to me the students have a pretty good deal out of this. They get a free ride to a good job on Rosinante and wind up eating better than they did in Texas."

"That isn't the point, Willy," said Bowman. "We don't give a shit about the students. The point is, the President wants old Luis Raul Panoblanco cut down a peg."

"So take him down a peg on charges of . . . oh, making a shuttle flight without a permit. Tax evasion. Mopery and dopery. Conspiracy to engage in mopery and dopery. What you've been talking begins to sound like political assassination, and I tell you it won't work."

"Violence is as American as cherry pie," said Schlecter.

"So it would be un-American not to waste the Governor of Texas?" asked Hulvey. "My God! He's fighting impeachment six ways to Sunday. He's got the classiest set of enemies in the whole country. What do you want to let him off the hook for?"

"Don't set yourself up to make judgments on the President," said Schlecter. "You don't know what all is going on."

"We need you on this one," wheedled Bowman, "you have to find us the way."

"Make a martyr of Panoblanco and you'll never be rid of him," said Hulvey. "I don't advise it."

"I want him dead," said the President.

"You do, do you?" replied Hulvey. "You trot me up to the mountaintop and say 'I want him dead,' do you? Well, God damn you, I won't do it! Get thee behind me, Mr. President Forbes, sir!"

Bowman polished his rimless glasses furiously.

"You weren't so fastidious about killing people in the past," he said. "The Creationist Crusade comes to mind. Some of the things happened then never did get cleaned up."

"Ain't it the truth," grinned Hulvey. "*I* can remember when you called it the Contra Darwin."

"I'm not threatening you," protested Bowman weakly, "I'm just trying to show you where your duty lies."

"Hey, Stan," said Hulvey gently, "*if* I killed anyone then, it was from Christian conviction. Do you think I'd kill like a hired thug now, when the big thug gives the word?"

"Don't be so fucking difficult, Hulvey!" snapped Schlecter. "This is your goddamned duty!"

"You're talking about *killing,* you bald-headed pimp! You're talking about *murder*! You tell me what my duty is, and you can't even say the *words*! I know you ain't never going to put it in writing, but you won't even *say* it!"

"Never argue with a Christian conscience, Bob," said President Forbes.

"Commissioner Hulvey. You have presented your case with great clarity and force. I have considered your argument. I have made my decision. A political necessity may be terribly wrong, but it is still a necessity. Now. Will you render unto Caesar what is Caesar's?"

There was a long pause.

"Not when he asks for what is God's," replied Hulvey at last. "I'm sorry, Mr. President."

"So am I, Mr. Hulvey. So am I. Please submit your resignation by close of business tomorrow." The President turned and stared at Administrator Bowman. "You too, Stanley," he said coldly.

The Administrator of NAUGA-Security looked stricken.

Hulvey took his card case out, wrote his resignation on the back of a business card, and handed it to Bowman.

"See that the President gets this in a timely fashion, Stan," he said.

Hulvey stood up.

"Good night, gentlemen, Mr. President."

At the door, the secret service agent joined him to make sure he found the exit.

"Mr. President," said Bowman unhappily, "I am positive that my resignation would not be in the National Interest at this time."

"You know what I want," said the President.

Not far from Asheville, North Carolina, is a small lake, on a quarter section of land that William Hulvey rented to his brother, who raised soy beans and maize. Bowman found Hulvey there, sitting in a fiberglass boat, fishing.

"Hey, Willy," he called from the shore, "why didn't you take your belt phone with you? You could have saved me the goddamn trip down."

"Didn't want to talk with nobody, Stan," was the calm reply. Bowman stood red-faced and flustered, brushing at gnats, until Hulvey finally switched on the battery-powered motor and crept over to the landing.

"What's on your mind, Stan?" he asked, looking up against the morning sun.

"Give me the rope," said Bowman. "I'll tell you when you get out of that damn boat." When the boat was made fast, Hulvey took a small string of fish out of the water and put them in the ice hamper with the beer. He handed the hamper up to Bowman, who took it with a grunt, and climbed on the landing.

"You is a bit out of shape, Stan," he said. "Now what's on your mind?"

"If you'd gone native on me, it would have been my cotton-pickin' mind," said Bowman. "I'm glad to see you still come to the point."

"I haven't been out of your sight one damn week and you're glad I come right to the point? Oh, Stan! What's up?"

"You put us in an awful fix, Willy, quitting like that." Bowman took out a handkerchief and mopped his forehead. "Sure is hot down here."

"You go air-conditioned all the way, what do you expect once you get outdoors?"

"I guess so, Willy. The President was madder'n hell, but I fixed things up for us."

"That's nice," said Hulvey. "What did you do?"

"I had Greene blow up Panoblanco, is what I did."

"Car bomb or mine?"

"You haven't heard? It's been on all the newscasts, all over the front pages—"

"I haven't heard zip since I came down here. What did you do?"

"Greene used a cruise missile—blew Panoblanco up when he was making a live broadcast on the TV."

"*A cruise missile!?*" Hulvey slammed his cap on the ground. "You fucking asshole! Who the fuck has cruise missiles except the fucking government?!"

"Now just you calm down, Willy. We had to work fast, but we covered our tracks real good, and as long as we run Security, nobody is going to get very far looking at them, either."

"I just bet you covered your goddamn tracks, Bowman, I'll bet you covered them with your goddamn business cards so nobody can't find nothing! A *cruise missile*, for Christ's sake!"

"Willy, it was work fast or be fired." Bowman picked up Hulvey's cap, dusted it off, and handed it back to him. "Forbes knows about the Contra Darwin, and he figures that's the way to keep the Mexican Independence movement in line."

"Well, he figures wrong," said Hulvey. "The Creationist Coalition raised enough money to get old Forbes the nomination, and they worked hard enough to elect the stupid bastard, but the rough stuff, the Contra Darwin, was maybe a dozen guys. When Joe Bob blew off Dr. Susan Brown, nobody stepped up to take her place. Once the von Zwang thing broke, the other side ran for cover, but how many of them were there? A few hundred is tops. Do you know how many Mexicans, Chicanos, Cubans, and miscellaneous Hispanics you have to deal with?" Bowman shook his head. "Well, if you took the trouble to find out you might be less eager to sic the Contra Darwin hit squad on them. You said you covered your tracks? I hope to God you're right, because I'll bet there's going to be a *lot* of enthusiasm to find the rascals that shot off that cruise missile."

"It's hot out here," said Bowman, blotting his forehead. "Isn't there someplace we can go sit down?"

"That's my camper over by the willow trees," said Hulvey. "I'll unfold the other chair and we can sit a spell." He picked up the hamper and walked along the edge of the lake, Bowman trailing a few paces behind.

"Your trouble, Willy, is you want to make things happen, you want to make policy," said Bowman. "The President, *he* makes policy. We're just there to make the wheels turn."

"Hey, Stan, you're the Administrator of NAUGA-Security—you're one of the wheels. You're *supposed* to be making policy."

"You know it, and I know it, but nobody's told the President yet."

"So go in and tell him," said Hulvey, setting the hamper down and unfolding an orange chair for his former chief.

"It isn't that easy, Willy," said Bowman. "You know what a temper he has. You cross him, he'll fire you in a minute."

Hulvey sat looking over the little lake. A fish jumped, making a notable splash in the silence.

"So he did," he said at last. "But you know what the job is, and you know how it ought to be done. You can at least do what you know is right instead of what you think the President wants."

"That's fine for you to say, Willy, but I worked hard to be somebody, and I'm not about to be throwing it away."

Hulvey took two cans of beer out of the hamper and handed one to Bowman.

"So you'll do what the man says?" He opened the can of beer with a slight spritz of foam. "Think about it, Bowman. How does *that* make you somebody?"

Bowman took off his glasses and polished them with his soggy handkerchief, smearing the lenses. He put them on, and they both laughed.

"Hey, Stan . . . you always *were* somebody. What's on your mind? You didn't come all the way down from St. Louis to make faces at me, did you?"

"No," said Bowman, "I wanted you back on the job, but you've been acting so goddamn self-righteous I don't know if I still do."

"Right," said Hulvey. He took a sip of beer and sat back in his chair to watch a blue kingfisher flashing over the water. After several minutes Bowman shrugged.

"Willy, I'm in too far to back out, and God knows, I'll need all the help I can get. You're damn near impossible to live with, but I can trust you, and you're competent, and I want you back. That's what I came for."

"Sure, Stan—I'll come back, but you know the rule: 'Never go back to a job you quit.' " Hulvey threw his empty beer can into the trash. "I'll go back as your deputy administrator."

"Be reasonable, Willy. That's a Presidential appointment."

"You think the Commissioner of the Military Intelligence Service is a civil service job, maybe? Tell the President you have to have me."

"I can't tell the President that."

"You don't have to have me?"

"I didn't say that. We've got to maneuver Hooke out of the job you want. It'll be reorganization time at central office, and the President goes along because that's the way it is. But it will take time."

"I'm in no hurry, Stan."

Dowman took off his glasses and looked at his handkerchief. "Too bad. Do you have some tissue?" He pulled a tissue from the package Hulvey offered him and wiped his glasses. "I'll talk to the President," he said at last. "At least wear your belt phone so I can call you up."

"It's in the camper," said Hulvey. "I just have to put the batteries back in."

From: The Executive Office
Subject: The Counterinsurgency Task Force (CTF)
To: NAUGA-Security
Date:

Since the assassination of Gov. Panoblanco there has been a serious increase in the level of banditry and terrorism among the Hispanic populations of the NAU. These elements have attempted to conceal their true nature by adopting slogans such as "Free Cuba," "Free Mexico," etc.

This problem poses a potential threat to the stability of the North American Union, and must be dealt with in a firm manner as expeditiously as possible.

Deputy Administrator Edwin A.J. Hooke is hereby detailed to head up the CTF. He is to be given every necessary assistance in this task so that the

CTF may be operational within 60 days of the date of this memorandum.

Attached is the CTF provisional budget.

By order of the President,

/s/

Robert Schlecter

Enclosure

CHAPTER 2

After several sleepless hours, William Hulvey put on his old blue bathrobe and went into the kitchen to brew himself a pot of tea. He ran water into the yellow melamine teapot, boiled it in the microwave oven, and added a spoonful of jasmine-scented tea leaves. While the tea was steeping, Corporate Elna, his personal computer, said:

"A Lieutenant Holt to see you. Shall I send him up?"

"It must be two in the morning," said Hulvey. "What does he want?"

"He said that it was urgent that he see you." Hulvey considered the matter. Holt was a good man, by and large. "So send him in."

Holt entered a few minutes later, a short blond man with large scarred hands, wearing a Navy raincoat over civilian clothes.

"Hello, Joe Bob," said Hulvey affably. "Will you have some tea?"

"Hey man, lay off the Joe Bob stuff. Old J.B. Baroody is on the lam forever. Call me Buck, if you want." Holt draped his raincoat over the back of one of the chairs and sat down. "Look. I killed a man a little while ago, and I want your office to see that it gets reported an accident or a suicide."

"Are you listening, Elna?" Hulvey asked.

"Yes. Do you want a transcript?"

"Yes. Go on, Buck."

"I pushed this fella in front of a subway train."

"Any witnesses?"

"A few. The usual eyes that see not. I was gone on a train headed the other direction in maybe twenty seconds. Fella named J. Willard Gibson."

"One such accident has been reported," said Corporate Elna, "but the victim has not yet been identified. This was about 2330 hours?"

"Was that it?" asked Hulvey. Holt/Baroody nodded. "You took your own sweet time getting here, didn't you?"

"Don't bug me, Willy! I stopped off for a couple of drinks is all."

"Why bother to come in at all, Buck? You could have called it in and got the same result."

"Ah, Willy . . . this one was different. I set the poor S.O.B. up for it. Do you have a beer?"

"In the fridge. How did you set him up?"

Holt opened the refrigerator and took out a brown bottle and a stein. He twisted the cap off and poured. "I went in pretending to be an MIS agent."

"Hell, Buck . . . that's what you do in real life. The Military Intelligence Service pays your damn salary, but I never see you."

"No, Willy—I mean I pretended to be another fella in the MIS and Gibson checked and found out I wasn't. First thing you know, some damn computer turned up old Joe Bob Baroody, and the sucker was in my way."

"So you took him out?"

"Yeah. He got in my way. But I feel bad about him. This fella was just a guy doing his job, not some goddamn creep scientist—he was just doing his job, and he backed into the goddamn buzzsaw." He sat and took a swallow of beer. "This is good stuff, Willy. Your own private label?"

"Yeah. I have my own microbrewery. How did Gibson put his nose in the way of your fist, Buck?"

"He has a client in the asteroids—a construction company that wanted a gene reader—and he put out a call for surplus equipment. The people at IBM told him to look for a surplus IBM GR/W-42, the only model they made that was maybe surplus."

"The asteroids, eh?" Hulvey sipped his tea thoughtfully. "That would be a legitimate reason to want one. The rate of defective live births is above six percent. But a 42? That's a research machine."

"He was looking for surplus, Willy . . . and God knows, we made the GR/W-42 surplus. The later machines are a lot simpler, but there's a six-month wait to get delivery." Holt finished his beer. "Look, maybe this is none of my business, but when was the last time you washed in the Blood of the Lamb?"

"It's been a while," conceded Hulvey. "Years in fact. Why do you ask?"

"Because I hurt," Holt said, "and in the old days I would have come to you and we'd pretty soon get to praying together. Now it's nothing but the facts, and butter won't melt in your mouth. *Why* aren't you keeping the faith?"

"Because the spirit doesn't move me anymore. Do you have what you need, Elna?"

"I think so," said the computer.

"The fix is in," said Hulvey. "Why don't you get on home to bed?"

"I don't want to go to bed. I feel real bad about that Gibson fella, and I want to get drunk. Only I daren't get drunk, so I came over here for some prayer, like in the old days. And you tell me the spirit don't move you no more! Why the hell not?!"

Hulvey finished his tea and sighed. "Because God has turned His face away from me. You're hurting, right? Well, I hurt, too. Let me tell you about it. I was in on the Contra Darwin from the very beginning; I helped set it up. One of the things I did was set up a double agent named Dr. Heinrich von Zwang in a lab to do a 'comparative study with chimpanzees and humans.' Okay? The deal was he was going to pretend to cross humans and chimps, and we'd expose him and put a stop to that whole goddamned line of research. Well, he lived up to his end of the bargain, all right, but he also really *did* cross humans and chimps. The word leaked out, and we had to move in on him before we were really set to go. I led the team that hit his lab. The monkey-babies—there were maybe a dozen, some in artificial wombs—we blew the hell out of them, but they looked human. And one of them—the oldest, I guess—could talk. She ran around the lab crying 'Don't hurt Jennie! Don't hurt Jennie!' and I grabbed her by the heels and smashed her head against the wall."

Hulvey walked to the refrigerator and took out a bottle of beer and the other stein. He uncapped the bottle on the wall opener and watched the foam rise as he poured the beer into the chilled glass. He took a swig of beer and sat down.

"She lay on the floor, bleeding at the mouth with one eye popped out of the socket, and I wondered if I hadn't made a mistake—she could have been my own kid, she looked that human. I was up when you came in because I'd been dreaming about her."

"Is that why you're a backslid sinner, Willy?"

"Not exactly, Joe Bob. What happened is that we nailed the whole goddamn genetic research community, and I wound up looking over one huge pile of grant applications to see who had tried to do what. Von Zwang was there. He had been trying everything you could think of to get his research funded, and those tight bastards wouldn't give him the time of day. It took me awhile to work it out, but I was the one that made von Zwang's work possible. And then it turned out that there was a notebook he kept. We destroyed maybe the last twenty, thirty pages with the damn lab, and we found the notebook carrier with von Zwang when we caught up with him two days later. We have an idea what he was doing from a paper he sent one of the journals. They knew hot stuff when they saw it, so they turned it in. We never did find the notebook . . . we traced it to a mail-forwarding service in Chicago. The best the fella could remember, it went to Cincinnati, and that was it." Hulvey finished his beer and set the stein on the table with a thump.

"Don't feel bad, Willy; that monkey-kid wasn't no way human."

"It isn't the killing that bothers me, Buck. What bothers me is that I'm responsible for her being created in the first place."

"Jesus will forgive you," Holt said.

Hulvey inspected his empty mug and smiled sadly. "Right," he said. "Old Stanley Bowman told me it was in a good cause, and I guess it was, and Jesus will forgive you for this Gibson fella. I have no doubt about it. I don't know what you were doing, but it was sure as hell in a good cause. See, Buck? You're feeling better already, ain't you?"

"Hey, I am, you know?"

"Good. Why don't you go on home and get some sleep, then?"

They shook hands, and Holt left.

Hulvey picked up the beer bottles and rinsed them out for reuse. He rinsed out the steins, wiping them dry with a dish towel, and replaced them in the refrigerator.

"Hey, Elna . . . we had a line on Gibson's office. Where did the response to his inquiry for a surplus GR/W-42 come from?"

"The Rockefeller Institute in Cincinnati."

"Cincinnati, eh? Did they offer to give him one?"

"No. They just asked what he wanted it for."

"I see." Hulvey nodded, and felt his growth of beard. "Well, we'll have to have someone look into it—the Institute, I mean."

"Shall I have Holt do it for you?"

"No. He's good and thorough, but the Rockefeller Institute is where he got tagged for that bombing in '34.

His ugly mug was posted all over the place and there's just too much chance he'd be spotted."

"What about Greene?"

"Hell, no! He can't chew gum and fart at the same time. When's my boy Dave coming back?"

"Friday a week. Do you want to wait that long?"

"Reckon we'll have to." Hulvey cleaned out the yellow teapot and put it in the dish rack with his teacup. "If they do have an IBM Gene Reader/Writer over there, it sure ain't going anyplace with Gibson dead, now, is it?"

"What about the people using it?"

"If it's there, we'll go after them. One of them might even have von Zwang's notebook."

"Mightn't they panic and destroy the evidence?"

"They might," Hulvey conceded with a yawn. "That would be almost as good as not doing it in the first place. Chances are, someone was just curious."

He turned out the kitchen light and went back to bed.

Lieutenant Commander David Riordan Hulvey was dozing in the VIP lounge of the Spokane airport when his belt phone rang. He snapped it open.

"Hulvey here," he said.

"St. Louis is returning your call at telecon booth six."

"I'll take it. Thanks."

He walked over to the booth and closed the door. The telecon screen was a maze of dancing colored dots, mostly reds and greens. He took out his encryption key and inserted it in the slot. The colors swirled around for a moment and then his father appeared in his St. Louis office.

"Hello, Dave."

"Hello, Dad. That's Dan, if it's not too much trouble. Or Riordan. Do you have a moment?"

"Sorry, Riordan. I'll make time. What have you found?"

"Some pretty strong inferences, as they say. From Cincinnati, the Rockefeller Institute sent a shipment with a 2,265-kilogram tare to Seattle via airfreight. It was routed via Spokane, where it went in and never came out. Okay? Two days later a shipment with a 2,265 tare, a UHRCAT Scanner from the Los Angeles Municipal Medical Center, went out as surplus equipment to a Navy pre-positioned hospital in the belt. That is, from Spokane, the shipment went to the Eastern Washington Shuttle Station, destination Laputa for transshipment to Mundito Rosinante, its ultimate destination. Okay? I checked with the Medical Center. They never sent any UHRCAT Scanner to surplus. They didn't send anything anywhere on the date in question. The number on the bill of lading was for a shipment of biological material they had sent to the Rockefeller Institute for calibration several months ago."

"So whatever it was is now on the way to Mundito Rosinante?" asked Hulvey, Senior.

"Right, Dad. Back in Cincinnati I talked to the shop crew and maintenance people at the Institute. They didn't know what they were moving—they didn't pack it—but they showed me the room it was moved from. I got the plat plan of the building, and the phone books back to '34, and checked to see who was in proximity to the room. From '34—that is, from the fall of '34—until the spring of '36 they had some of their top computer architects close by. And theoreticians. Dr. Maxwell Stanton had an office across the hall—the man who worked out the R-complex structure analogs for computers."

"Worked *at* it, at any rate," the senior Hulvey remarked sourly. "He undoubtedly has the reputation. Go on."

"From the spring of '37 on, the room was occupied by a device that was incorporated as Corporate Susan Brown, a wholly owned subsidiary of the Rockefeller Institute."

"And on the third year she arose from the dead?"

"What, Dad?"

"Dr. Susan Brown was killed in August of '34 when the bomb that took out her IBM GR/W-42 went off. That's the one they tagged Joe Bob with."

"Right. I checked the record on Corporate Susan Brown, to see if it quoted her specs. All it said was: 'hybrid experimental model.' So I copied the serial numbers and checked with IBM. They said it incorporated elements of the GR/W-42, but that they couldn't say what it was being used for without some idea of the software and firmware involved. One fella volunteered the opinion that there was an unusual amount of redundancy in the listed equipment. I asked him if the list was complete, and he said that with experimental models you often find as much as twenty or twenty-five percent of the total circuitry is tailor-made."

"That's interesting, Dave. Riordan. You did a good job."

"Thanks, Dad."

"Was there anything else?"

"The Rockefeller Institute is a bunch of unrepentant sinners." They both laughed.

"You think the flight of Corporate Susan Brown is a case of the wicked flee when no man pursueth?"

"No, Dad. The timing is off."

"Oh?" Hulvey, Senior, looked at his watch. "How do you figure?"

"This fella Gibson made an inquiry, right? Okay. The Institute made a very guarded response. When they learned it was off-planet, the Institute vested title *in* Corporate Susan Brown *with* Corporate Susan Brown, and she moved within hours of the news of Gibson's death hitting the papers. The work order moving her out had to be processed at least a day or two before. The work crew didn't indicate that the move was anything other than routine. So it wasn't panic flight, it had to be something else. Did I tell you I tried to find out what work Susie B. was doing?"

"What was she doing?"

"I couldn't find out."

"How hard did you look?"

"Hard enough. The machine is not only not credited in any of the Institute's publications, it isn't even *mentioned*. It was just there." The younger Hulvey smiled. "I went through the budget to see how it was funded. Okay? There was nothing, no line item, not in '34. Not in '35. Not in '36. The Institute was running a major project on volunteer labor and fat from the budget. You want my opinion?"

"Yes. What do you make of it, Riordan?"

"We hit them hard to make them stop, and instead of stopping they went underground." The elder Hulvey shook his head.

"They stopped. Since the Contra Darwin, manipulation of human genes is dead. Even screening for birth defects—which is what Gibson was asking about—is pretty stagnant."

"They ain't dead. They haven't published, is all. Furthermore—"

"Excuse me, Commissioner," said Corporate Elna, "the Administrator is on the other line."

"—I'll bet she has von Zwang's notebook."

"Maybe so, son. I have to go now. God bless you." They broke the connection simultaneously.

RECORD OF MEETING

Time: 27 November, '40   1330—1605 hrs.
Place: Temporary Building #113, Rm. 409
Subject: Implementation of Pending Declaration of Martial Law
Present: Bob Schlecter, Executive Office
              Edwin A.J. Hooke, NAUGA-Security, CTF
              Wm. M. Hulvey, NAUGA-Security, Deputy Administrator
              J. Walter Bland, Jr. NAUGA-Justice, Deputy Administrator
              VAdm. Peter Dugas, NAVY-Security
              RAdm. Raoul Flores, NAVY-Security

MGen. D.S. Mueller, ARMY-Security
BGen. Vivian Barfield, ARMY-Security

Ed Hooke opened the meeting with a prayer, and continued to dispense pious bullshit for the next two and one-half hours. The imposition of martial law, it appears, is PRESIDENTIAL POLICY because "banditry and terrorism" (taking in vain the fair name of "Hispanic Nationalism") has increased markedly following the unfortunate demise of Gov. Panoblanco. Who would have thought it?

He looked me in the eye and said: "The President wants team players, Hulvey. Men who will implement his policies!" I said I would, of course, implement the President's policies, but didn't he think that a limited decree of emergency powers might not be a better way of achieving the same objective? He said absolutely not! I said: There is nothing on this checklist that couldn't be done under a limited-emergency-powers decree, and did the President have something in mind that he wasn't telling us? He said: No, it was all up front, and then Bland tore him up. I believe he talked ten minutes without taking a breath. I asked him about it afterward, and he said they taught him staggered breathing in law school. Anyway, *absolutely not* became *refer the matter back to the President*. Schlecter said: "Do you think a limited decree is the way to go, Hulvey?" and when I said yes, he said: "That's how we'll do it, then." Hooke was really mad.

Flores said the checklist appeared to be mostly anti-Hispanic measures. Hooke said most of the banditry and terror was by Hispanics. So Flores asked if there would be a purge of Hispanic naval officers, similar to the purge of the (mostly Anglo) "Old Regimists" in '31–'32. Hooke waffled around until Schlecter cut him off with a flat no.

Dugas complained about the political officers' dogmatism and lack of technical competence, and suggested that computers might do a better job. Bar field suggested that filaments might be even better. Schlecter said that political officers will have to have advanced technical training before being promoted in the future. Mueller said this idea had been around for years, were they finally going to do it? Hooke complained that the meeting was getting off the subject, and asked if there were any comments on the checklist. There was some discussion of logistics, and then he looked at me and said: "Do *you* have any questions, Mr. Hulvey?"

So I said, well, as long as we're cracking down on the Panoblancos and all their works, there is this joint project by Scadiwa—the Southern California Agricultural Desalinated Water Authority, which is down on the list as a notorious hotbed of Panoblancos—and Mitsui, which is undoubtedly a conduit for Japanese gold going to Hispanic bandits and terrorists, and are we going to deal with it? Hooke looked properly stern and said yes, of course we are, and isn't it on the list? And I said it isn't on the list. It's out in the asteroids, and its name is Mundito Rosinante. He said it wouldn't make any difference, and I said fine, will the Navy look into it for us?

Flores said they'd have to check the budget before they could give me a firm answer. Schlecter told him to find the money. Flores said it was a question of finding a ship that could be pulled off-station for 100–120 days without breaking down, and it might be a month or two before one could be scheduled. Dugas said that that seemed to be a lot of trouble to take for one or two individuals, and I told him that we'd extend them an invitation to visit Laputa first, but if they refused to go, would the Navy fetch them for us? I quoted Hooke about team players. Dugas said that if they didn't come, the Navy would certainly consider sending a ship for them. Schlecter said they damn well better send that ship. Dugas asked who we wanted to arrest and I told him we didn't know yet, but we'd keep him posted. He asked if we'd send along an observer, and I said fine, we'd

do that thing. Probably we'll send along Lieutenant Holt, although I didn't say so. That was about it.
Signature block
Copies to: Administrator, Commissioner-MIS, File.
Classification: 90 days Secret, print in noncopying mode.

Hulvey studied the record of the meeting on the display screen.

"That's pretty good," he told Corporate Elna. "Take out the reference to Lieutenant Holt—it isn't relevant. And maybe you ought to take out the jokes."

"I thought requiring technical training for political officers was an important development," Elna said.
Hulvey rubbed his jaw thoughtfully.

"You may be right," he conceded. "It could be a way to finesse Dave's next promotion. Leave the jokes in."

The display screen faded slowly into blankness, and his desk pushed the meeting report at him for his signature, perfectly typed with justified margins, pale blue ink on crisp, Day-glo white bond.

Hulvey signed it, attached the buck slip, and put it in his Out box.

CHAPTER 3

Date: 8 December '40
From: Edwin A.J. Hooke, CTF
Subject: Panoblanco Files in re Mundito Rosinante
To: William M. Hulvey, Deputy Administrator

In accordance with your memorandum dated December 2, 2040, we have conducted a thorough search of the Panoblanco files seized on December 1 for evidence supporting the prosecution of individuals involved with Mundito Rosinante at the construction site.

A careful review leads to the conclusion that no such prosecution is warranted. The reviewed documents are forwarded in microfiche as Attachment I.

The allegation that Mundito Rosinante might in some way have served as a conduit for Japanese money directed to Hispanic nationalists has also been investigated. The Panoblancos appear to have made substantial profits in the space-construction speculation whose recent collapse brought down the Ecufiscale Tellurbank. These profits are derived from Rosinante only insofar as the Panoblancos defaulted on loans made by the Tellurbank with Rosinante given as security. Attachment II is a financial flow chart of the Panoblanco financial empire. Mundito Rosinante was never of central importance, and since the default, has been associated with neither Mitsui nor the Panoblancos.

It is appropriate to reiterate that no proper prosecution can be supported by the evidence at hand. If you wish to have your own people review the Panoblanco files, simply use the CTF encryption plus ENTRY P-File.

/s/
Edwin A.J. Hooke

Dolores Ferranes, Director of the Legal Division of NAUGA-Security, set her cobra ashtray on Hulvey's conference table and plugged it in. The coils of the cobra collected the ashes, and the fangs in its open mouth were made of stainless steel bristles that provided a deodorizing flow of oxygen ions.

Dolores rolled a tobacco cigarette and lit it.

"Hooke's right," she said, exhaling smoke. "I had Cooper going over it from one direction and Krauss going over it from the other." She put her briefcase beside the ashtray and opened it, spreading out file folders in gay profusion on the conference table. "There is nothing going on at the construction site that calls for us to pay Mundito Rosinante a visit."

"That's too bad," said Hulvey.

"The best they came up with was to pull in the project manager on suspicion—fellow named Cantrell." She picked up one of the folders. "Charles Chavez Cantrell."

"So go ahead. Is there any problem?"

"He's pretty clean. If you picked him up, like he was already in custody, you could hold him a few days." She flicked ash into her cobra. "No problem. Try to hold him a few weeks, his lawyer will sure as hell get him released. You want to send a ship out to get him, I don't think we can swing it."

"What do we know about him—Cantrell?"

Ferranes riffled through the folder, finally extracting a sheet of paper.

"Our boy was a space-engineering major at Indiana University, graduating June 2018 with a B.S.E. and an NROTC ensign's commission. Listed as fluent in Spanish and Japanese." She blew a smoke ring, and pulled out another page. "He extended his enlistment one year to get a space assignment. Outstanding performance ratings, politically not so good—one satisfactory, two acceptables, one unacceptable, reversed on appeal. He was denied promotion after he married a Japanese national, and resigned his commission on August 5, '22."

"He was denied a lieutenantcy?" Hulvey asked.

"No, he *was* a lieutenant. He was up for lieutenant commander."

"Interesting," he said. "Why did he get an unacceptable political rating?"

"Because the P.O. said he was sympathetic to the Old Regime."

"And it was reversed?"

"This was '22, remember," replied Ferranes. "They were taking a much softer line back then."

"Right," said Hulvey. "Did he have any kids?"

"No, they separated and were divorced a year later."

Dolores Ferranes put out her cigarette and deliberately rolled another one, lighting it with a thumb-struck match.

"Cantrell is a *long* ways off," she said, "and there is no rational reason to go after him. Is this Contra Darwin business?"

"Ye-es. At least it may be. Dave thinks the von Zwang notebook went out there very recently. The Rockefeller Institute rebuilt the GR/W-42 that was blown up in '34. Dave makes a pretty good case that they did it to continue working on human genetics. The machine went to Rosinante, and Dave thinks the notebook may have gone with it."

"Dave is pretty sharp," she agreed. "Why does he think so?"

"Among other things, the Rockefeller Institute incorporated their machine under the name of Susan Brown."

"Corporate Susan Brown?"

Hulvey nodded.

"That *is* suggestive, I must admit," said Ferranes, exhaling smoke. "Okay then, the way to go is to invite Cantrell in to answer unspecified charges that we *never* specify. He won't come. I wouldn't come either, if I were him. And eventually we have to go get him."

"That's pretty raw," said Hulvey, watching the ions from the snake's fangs eating the slowly rising smoke. "But I can't think of anything better. So we'll do it. Poor bastard, he'll never know what hit him."

The first disquieting news from Rosinante was indirect. Dolores Ferranes did a routine search of NAU court cases involving Mundito Rosinante, and turned up Joseph Marino *vs.* the NAU, a conviction of murder in the first degree. Ferranes was curious and she was thorough. She went in to see Deputy Administrator Hulvey two days later.

"You *will* have trouble with Cantrell," she told him,

setting her briefcase, handbag, and ashtray on the conference table. "He maybe used to be a hired hand for the contractor, but times, Mr. Hulvey, have changed." She plugged in the cobra ashtray. "To begin with, he holds majority control of Mundito Rosinante," she slid a paper out of one of the file folders, "and he has been elected Governor of the same."

"Governor, Dolores?" Hulvey scowled. "Who the hell is out there to vote for him?" She opened a second folder and began leafing through it.

"Here," she said. "At the last count, there were 5,182 workers and dependents, union and management, 2,491 students transported *en corvée* from the Alamo—of whom 55 later went home—and 2,501 young ladies sent up from Japan." She paused. "A footnote says they were Koreans, for all the difference it makes. You have in excess of ten thousand people, and while that wouldn't carry much weight on the south side of Chicago, it constitutes a respectable population out in the asteroids." She took matches, tobacco pouch, and cigarette papers out of her purse and set them on the table. "Mundito Rosinante, Mr. Hulvey, is a political entity, and you maybe ought to treat it with respect." She rolled herself a cigarette and lit it, striking the match with her thumbnail.

"The trouble is," she continued, exhaling smoke, "that you focused on Corporate Susan Brown one hundred percent, and didn't look at anything else. Why did she go there anyway, do you think?"

"Perhaps she felt we were closing in on her," Hulvey suggested.

"Not likely, Mr. Hulvey. I suspect she went because she wanted to go." She flicked ash into the cobra's coiled body and pulled out another paper. "Take a look at what her equipment was, according to the serial numbers from her incorporation papers. Medical equipment. Diagnostic equipment. Surgical equipment. It had the capability to become a first-class hospital, and out in the asteroids, that is exactly what it is becoming."

"Well, that is just too goddamned bad," said Hulvey,

"because I strongly suspect that she—it—has the von Zwang notebook. The missing one."

"So," said Ferranes, blowing a smoke ring. "You are going after her. Only you can't, because the Contra Darwin is illegal. So you have to feint at Cantrell to thrust at Corporate Susan. What I'm telling you is: it may be dangerous to feint at Cantrell—especially if you startle him."

"Maybe so," Hulvey conceded, "but we don't have to startle him to get at her. At it."

"Perhaps, but you ought to know what you'll be going up against, Mr. Hulvey. You knew the Navy is putting in a Class Two Repair Base with a prepositioned hospital?"

"Hell yes, it was the request for surplus equipment that touched this whole thing off in the first place."

"Right," she flicked ash at the cobra. "Did you see the report that Captain Phillipe Ryan submitted?"

"Come on, Dolores, that's what I have you for. What did he say?"

"He went out to take the Alamo corvée home. By the time he got there, the Government having moved with its usual glacial swiftness, Mitsui had sent up those Japanese girls, and nobody wanted to leave home for Texas. Ryan is the kind that obeys orders without question, and he would have had the Marines go in and load up the Alamo corvée at gunpoint—his report says as much—except that Cantrell had these three companies of students—former students, anyway—deputized as Texas state troopers and armed with the old-model Stangl rifles." She put out her cigarette. "I expect they have the new model by this time."

"Well, so what? Push comes to shove, we can stand off Mundito Rosinante and threaten to use *Force Majeure,* and the infantry can't do a damn thing."

"Can you, now?" Ferranes rolled another cigarette and lit it. "You can threaten, but what if the other side sits tight and calls . . . oh, say, Senator Gomez for help? What will you tell him when he asks you why you are going to kill all those people?" She pulled another folder out of her briefcase, and took a paper from it. "And if the shooting starts, you might just possibly lose your damn ship." She pushed the paper at him. "Ryan was very worried about the safety of *his* ship because Mundito Rosinante was built with a Mitsubishi Dragon Scale Mirror." Hulvey ignored the paper she had pushed at him.

"What the hell is a Mitsubishi Dragon Scale Mirror?"

"It's a third-generation stationary array of mirrors," said Ferranes, drawing on her cigarette. "Basically it's a field of several million mirrors two to three meters in diameter, each mirror being able to rotate on its axis, and each axis being able to rotate on a track that is set in the plane of the field." She set her pen upright on one of the papers and began to turn it. Then she stuck a cigarette paper under the clip. "Okay, the cigarette paper is the mirror, and the pen rotates around its axis, see? But the axis can also rotate." She turned the pen so that it was parallel to the table, and then rotated the pen with the cigarette paper. "Each mirror is guided by a chip. It can be programmed to follow a daily or yearly routine, or you can broadcast a location and orchestrate the mirror array to provide process heat. *Or* you could use it as a weapon to melt holes in a spaceship at a distance of several thousand kilometers. Those are the specifications."

Hulvey took the paper she had offered him earlier and glanced at it briefly. "Japanese Navy design?" he said softly. "That must be the Mitsui connection. Go on."

"So much for *Force Majeure*," Ferranes said, exhaling smoke. "Now you might say: 'Oh, Cantrell—*he's* just a country boy!' "

Hulvey smiled in spite of himself. Whenever he would propose something of dubious legality and low cunning, he would remark: "Now *I'm* just a country boy."

"So perhaps," she continued, "you might want to try *Force Chicane*. You know about the Federal judge on Rosinante?" Hulvey laughed.

"Okay, Dolores—tell me about the Federal judge. Cantrell owns him lock, stock, and barrel?"

"No. Judge Corporate Skaskash was owned by the Econometric Institute of Kiev and the Ecufiscale Tellurbank. It now holds majority control of itself."

"A judicial computer, eh? We might have trouble with *Force Chicane* at that," Hulvey conceded. "How did it happen?"

"They needed a judge for a murder trial," Ferranes said, "so Skaskash passed the qualifying tests and got elected the same time as Cantrell was being elected Governor. When it isn't being a judge, it is under contract to Cantrell, so I expect that if it *can* rule in his favor it *will*." She exhaled smoke. "I would suggest that for anything less than the certainty of locating von Zwang's notebook you do not bother. The risk is very high."

Hulvey sat back and studied Dolores Ferranes for a few minutes. She should let the natural gray show in her hair, he thought. The black tint she used made her face look harsh and forbidding.

"You may be right," he said at last. "The downside of the operation could be pretty bad."

"Do you want to cancel? It would be no problem to call it off at this point."

"I don't think so, Dolores. We maybe ought to change our plan a little, is all. Instead of blowing Cantrell away and picking off Corporate Susie B in the general confusion, suppose we feint at him with one hand and hit Corporate Susie with the other?"

"And then call the whole thing off from here," she nodded, flicking ash at her cobra. "That should work. My question is: How are you going to write the orders to the P.O.? I assume a Political Officer will be in charge?"

"Yes. Yes, we'll have to have a P.O. in charge. Holt can do the dirty work, but he can't run the operation.

And we can't tell an outsider what we're up to, so it'll have to be a two-man operation. Dave would be good, but I can't use him for something like this. Too close to home. Who else do we have?"

"Judge Purvis would be good. What about him?"

"He's up for re-election this fall, Dolores. How about Billy Lee Prowse?"

"How about him? He's managing Reverend Daugherty's *Hour of Salvation* program. He's big time now. Do you think he'd go?"

"No," Hulvey shook his head. "Not for as long as we'd be needing him. I suppose there's always Greene."

"Good old Homer Greene," said Ferranes. "Are you *sure* you don't want to cancel out?"

"No, I ain't—aren't," he said, "but this thing has been gnawing at my soul for a long time. And Greene's a lieutenant colonel in NAVY-Security. He's beautifully placed to move into the P.O.'s slot."

"If you give him a good thorough briefing I suppose you can trust him not to foul up the detail?" she said doubtfully, exhaling smoke.

"If there is a way, Greene will find it," said Hulvey. "But this should be right up his alley—bluster and bluff and do absolutely nothing without word from me. What could go wrong?" Ferranes stubbed out her cigarette and began gathering up her papers.

"I don't know. If I knew, we could do something about it. And Holt is there for Greene to consult, so the downside shouldn't be *too* bad." She closed her briefcase with a snap and unplugged her ashtray. "I would have to say the risk is acceptable."

"I'll sleep on it," he said as they walked to the door, "but I expect that we'll do it."

"In that case, I'll put the package together for you so you can take it in to Bowman at lunch tomorrow. You think he'll buy it?"

"Oh, hell yes," said Hulvey.

CHAPTER 4

Corcoran's Apartment Hotel is in one of the run-down sections of St. Louis, near the Pruitt-Igoe Subway Station. On the ground floor of the hotel is Danny the Cork's Irish Pub, a sit-down vending machine decorated with plastic shamrocks and travel posters. Push the buttons on the menu, your order lights up, and your total bill appears. Insert cash in the pneumatic tube—you can hear the coins rattle—and presently a robot rolls along the ceiling track to serve your order. Your change, if any, comes back via tube.

Lieutenant Oscar James Holt, a.k.a. Joe Bob Baroody, sat in a back booth with a beer and a newspaper. He wore the khaki fatigue uniform of the NAU Navy, with the light blue tabs of the political service on the shoulder. A regular Navy rating might notice that he looked a bit overage in grade, but would remark on the fact with a certain discretion if at all. As he finished his beer, he was joined by Lieutenant Commander Hulvey.

"You're late, Dan," Holt said without looking up.

"The review board was running late," said Hulvey. "It's a formality, but I had to be there. What's good?"

"They have fresh mussels," said Holt. "The paper says Security cracked down on the Panoblancos, finally. I suppose that's good, too."

Hulvey pushed the buttons for steamed mussels and fettuccine and a beer. "You want a refill?" Holt nodded, and Hulvey pressed for two beers and put a bill in the tube. "The country is coming apart at the seams and you suppose that's good, do you? The country's headed for a civil war."

"Well, that's good for Security, isn't it? Come on, Dan, if things get too quiet, we might have to look for work." He swallowed the heeltap that remained in his mug. "How did the review board go?"

"Oh, I passed all right. What's new with you?"

"You heard we got a line on the von Zwang notebook?" Hulvey nodded. "Well, I been assigned to the NAUSS *Ciudad Juárez,* which will be going out to the asteroids to pick up stray Panoblancos, and one of our stops is Mundito—ah, Mundito Rosenbaum."

"Mundito Rosinante," said Hulvey.

"Right. I knew a girl named Muñeca Rosenbaum, once—anyway, Homer Greene is going along to front for me, and I'm going to see about this Corporate Susan Brown, who is the odds-on favorite to have the von Zwang notebook."

"How did it get to be odds-on?" asked Hulvey. The waiter robot rolled up with their order, which it lowered on a tray. They removed the beer and food, and the waiter robot raised the tray with Holt's empty mug and rolled off.

"What was I talking about?" asked Hulvey between bites.

"You had just passed the review board. What then?"

"Right. I've been promoted to Commander, once I complete the twelve-week missile course."

"Hey, that's great, Dan!" Holt raised his beer in a toast, and Hulvey joined him. "San Diego?"

"No, Havana. Originally it was going to be out in the L-4s somewhere, I would have liked that. Hey, these mussels are very nice."

"That's what they told me," Holt said. "Don't you mean 'will be promoted'?"

"No, my promotion is effective as of December 1, conditional on passing the missile course." He took a drink of beer. "I might have been promoted? No, my daddy wouldn't stand for that. I've got to take the course, but there is no way I'm not going to pass it, and

I have *been* promoted. How do you feel about going into space, Buck?"

"I never been there, but what the hell—" he took a drink of beer. "Maybe I can find me a nice place to settle down, once this Corporate Susan Brown thing gets squared away. Hey, if you've been promoted, that calls for a celebration! What about a pretty girl?"

"I could do with a pretty girl, about now," Hulvey said. He finished his fettuccine and touched a button on the menu. "What about my change?" he asked.

"Coming right up, sir," said a voice. "All you have to do is whistle. You know how to whistle, don't you?"

"You just pucker up your lips and blow," said Holt and Hulvey in unison.

The change rattled in the pneumatic tube, and two underclass girls, skinny, fifteen or sixteen, walked up.

"Lonely, honey?" one of them asked.

Hulvey patted the seat beside him. "Sit down, poontang," he said, and the girl sat down beside him, her companion squeezing in next to her, giggling.

"Why not 'New in town, sailor'?" asked Holt.

" 'Cause you mens is regulars," said the second.

"See what you get for living in a fleabag like Corcoran's?" said Hulvey.

"It beats the hell out of the Bachelor Officer's Quarters," replied Holt. "Hey, honey, why don't you come and sit by my side, little darling?" The girl on the outside came over and sat beside him. He put his arm around her.

"Now you stop feeling that thing!" she said.

"Right," said Hulvey, "let's go over to the Metropole. No point in fooling around in a bar when you could be fooling around in a Jacuzzi."

The Stargate Motel is within view of the main gate of the Baja Shuttle Base and the Pacific Ocean. Lieutenant Colonel Homer Greene leaned forward and tapped his driver on the shoulder.

"Honey," he said, "pull off into the motel yonder, I could badly use a little nap."

"It's only 1630, sir," she said, slowing down to make a left turn into the motel.

"That's *your* time, honey. I flew in from Gander, Newfoundland, for this morning's conference in St. Louis, from where I took a commercial flight to San Diego to make connection with *you*. I figure it is about midnight when I didn't get no sleep the night before." She pulled into the motel and he walked into the office with his official credit card. He inserted it in the slot, and the machine dropped a key on the desk.

"Thank you for your patronage, Colonel Greene. Have you any special instructions?"

"Why, sure," he said. "I'm due out on the 2140 shuttle, so I'd appreciate a call at about 2000 or so."

"Of course, sir," said the motel. "Please sign the bill." He signed the paper the motel pushed at him, and the motel took the signed bill and disgorged his credit card. He walked back to the car.

"Shall I take your bags, sir?" asked his driver.

"Just the small one," he told her.

Once inside the room he sent her out for some ice, and by the time she came back with the bucket, he had taken out a bottle of bourbon and removed his shoes. He put ice cubes in two glasses and poured out two shots.

"I'm on duty, sir," protested his driver, "I really shouldn't be drinking."

"Drink your drink, kick off your shoes, and watch the nice movie, young trooper," said Greene. "And that's an order." The tone of voice carried conviction, and after a moment's hesitation she obeyed. The motel's color TV had a cassette player, and Greene had put on a pornographic film he had picked up in St. Louis.

Afterward, when she was taking a shower, she heard him cry out. She turned off the water and walked into the bedroom, toweling her close-cropped blond hair. He was stretched out on the unmade bed, wearing her uniform.

"Chest hurts," he gasped. "Can't breathe. Get—get help . . ."

She picked up the phone and called the base hospital. While she was talking, he gave a convulsive shudder and a cry that was clearly audible over the phone. A helicopter ambulance arrived presently, to find the late Homer Greene already set in rigor. The crew took him and the driver (who had slipped on his shirt and pants) to the base hospital, where heroic methods to restart the heart were employed without success. Lieutenant Colonel Homer Greene was pronounced dead about the same time the motel was giving his room the requested wake-up call.

NAVY-Security, upon being informed, examined Greene's mission, compared the psychological profiles of available officers and selected Major Gerald Terry as his replacement. Since Major Terry was already on Laputa, the computer gave Greene's seat on the shuttle to the senior noncom on standby. It was not felt necessary to consult with NAUGA-Security, let alone William Hulvey, since neither of them were formally associated with the mission, and were not, therefore, in the chain of command.

Deputy Administrator Hulvey learned of the event three days later, when Greene's widow asked him to be a pallbearer at her husband's funeral. By then, of course, any window during which the mission might have been canceled was closed, and Lieutenant Oscar James Holt, a.k.a. Joe Bob Baroody, was on his own.

The day after the NAUSS *Ciudad Juárez* docked at Mundito Rosinante, William M. Hulvey arrived at his office around noon. The painters were finished, but the odor of latex paint was heavy in the air. The "old" carpeting—it had been installed less than a year earlier for Hooke, the then Deputy Administrator—had been taken up and was piled in huge rolls out in the hall. Inside, workers were applying mastic and laying random-width hardwood flooring with simulated pegs over the concrete floor. Hulvey stood watching them for a few minutes.

"How soon will you be finished?" he asked.

"You ought to be able to move in late afternoon, sir," said the foreman, "tomorrow A.M. at the latest."

"That's good." Hulvey had moved into the Deputy Administrator's office when he was named to the job on an acting basis, but he hadn't done any redecorating until his appointment had been formally confirmed. Now the room would bear his stamp. Georgetown-blue walls. Oyster-white fiberglass drapes figured with a white silk pattern. A wooden floor with a custom woven area rug. Junk and stuff to show how important he was. The drapes and rug were stashed in the receptionist's office, a Qing vase more than a meter tall sat on her desk. Its mate sat on the credenza behind her. He hung up his hat and coat and walked out.

"I'll be over in the legal office," he told the girl.

"Nothing much going on right now," said Ferranes, flicking ash into the coils of the cobra ashtray. "The ongoing investigation of Old Regimists in the Navy is on hold, and the Hispanic revolutionists seem to have gone on vacation. How was Havana?"

"Beautiful," Hulvey said. "Dave graduated first in his class athletically *and* scholastically, so I rented a boat and we went deep-sea fishing. We each caught a marlin, and Dave caught a fair-sized sailfish—if I had caught it, it would have been gigantic." He put a tea bag in a plastic cup and ran hot water on it. "The sea was *so* beautiful, deep blue, and clear, and just rough enough to let you know it was still alive—not choppy at all." He took the tea bag out for a second and put it back to steep some more. "And on the way in, we had the most incredible sunset. Reds and golds like you wouldn't believe, and on the edges mauve and purples and the most incredible clear green luminous sky. That's how I'd like to decorate my office, Dolores."

"Did you pin the Commander's insignia on Dave?"

"I gave him a set, fourteen-karat-gold-filled, but no, I didn't put them on. Dave—Riordan he prefers—is a grown man. But I told him how proud I was of him."

"Very good," said Ferranes, stubbing out her cigarette. "You should be proud of him."

"He told me something. When he had time free from his studies, he went over the files on the von Zwang episode. He read the original raw transcript of the interrogation of the fellow who ran the mail drop."

"Where we lost the trail?" she asked.

"Right. The man was under hypnosis to aid his recall. He was, you might say, cooperating under duress. Anyway, he didn't remember, and he didn't remember, and finally our man says to him: 'Was it sent to the Rockefeller Institute in Cincinnati?' and the response was: 'I think it was sent to Cincinnati.' "

"Shit! Who was the asshole doing interrogation—Greene?"

"I asked him the same thing. Dave just laughed and said it was water over the dam. We docked about then, and I let the matter drop. It *is* over the dam, you know. Greene's dead."

"We're sending a ship out to the asteroids because of a response to a leading question, Mr. Hulvey?" said Ferranes. "We're taking serious risks and wasting money on the basis of a sloppy, half-assed job like *that*? And the shithead doctored the transcript so *he* would look better! Jesus Christ!"

"It's the only clue we have," said Hulvey calmly, "and knowing what we know about Corporate Susie B., do you think we could just ignore her?"

"Probably not, no." Dolores fingered her coral necklace thoughtfully. "Potentially, she—it has the ability to conduct genetic research on humans and no visible inhibitions about doing so. I guess we have to check her out, whether we like it or not."

"Check her out, hell! Holt is going to trash her!"

"Holt's able, but too violent. Couldn't we have sent someone else?" She took out her makings and rolled a cigarette.

"We discussed that. If Baroody wasn't in hiding, we wouldn't even have Holt." He frowned. "You smoke too much."

Dolores struck a kitchen match on her thumbnail. "Damn right," she said, lighting up. "A dirty, expensive habit, but mine own. Unlike terrorism in a holy cause, however, it isn't illegal." She blew a smoke ring. "The asteroids are a long way off, Mr. Hulvey, and if you didn't think Corporate Susie might have von Zwang's stuff, would you have gone after her?"

"You want out of the Contra Darwin?"

"How in God's name could I get out if I wanted to?" she asked. "What I want to know is: are we going to act like hot-eyed zealots forever?"

"No," he said, "but I like to do a proper job on anything I tackle."

"Bullshit, Mr. Hulvey, sir. Answer my question." Hulvey's belt phone rang.

"Lt. Holt arrived at Mundito Rosinante as of 1303 hours yesterday," said Corporate Elna, "and his report is going through the decoding section. Will you want to see it?"

"Yes, of course. Hard copy soonest well, my desk is temporarily out in the hall." He took a swallow of his lukewarm tea. "Put the hard copy on the priority list. I'll take it at home, if necessary." He snapped the phone shut. "What was the question, Dolores?"

She took a deep drag on her cigarette and exhaled the smoke through her nostrils. "Doesn't it bother you that your fate hangs on good old Holt being lucky?"

"Not really," he said, "I haven't dreamed of Jennie since the operation began."

The next day, Hulvey sat in on a teleconference of the Regional Security Administrators discussing current problems. It was well into the third hour, and they were rehashing a technical question: whether the broadcasts put out by Adelita Blanquista originated from a moving source in the regions where they were heard, or whether they were rebroadcast via satellite from some more distant point of origin.

Hulvey unfolded a keyboard in his lap and typed out: ANYTHING NEW ON THE MISSION TO ROSINANTE?

On the reading screen the answer floated up: YES. WE HAVE A REQUEST FROM MAJOR TERRY, THE P.O. ON THE NAUSS *Ciudad Juárez,* FOR PERMISSION TO ADVISE C.C. CANTRELL OF THE CHARGES AGAINST HIM. WE HAVE A REPORT FROM LT. HOLT SAYING THAT HE HAS LOCATED CORPORATE SUSAN BROWN. AND WE HAVE A PHONE CALL FROM SEN. GOMEZ'S OFFICE . 'ON THE MATTER OF CHARLES CHAVEZ CANTRELL.'

I'LL TAKE THE PHONE CALL, he typed out, KEEP MY FACE STRAIGHT ON THE TELECON SCREEN, ELNA. After a moment his belt phone sounded. He snapped it open.

"Deputy Administrator Hulvey, NAUGA-Security, returning your call," he said.

"Why, that's right kind of you," said a woman's voice, "I'm Maria Yellowknife, in Senator Gomez' office." The apostrophe ess on *Gomez's* was slurred into the zed in a Western accent that Hulvey couldn't place.

"You're not from Texas," he said. "I know most of the Texican dialects. Where do you come from?"

"Mexico City," she said, "but I went to school at Cambridge, that's the one in England, of course, not the one in Texas. Look, we have a constituent named Cantrell. Are you familiar with him?"

"Corporate Elna brought me up to date on the file," said Hulvey.

"Good. Our man is out in the asteroids, about as far away from all this fuss about Mexican Independence as can be imagined. There he is, minding his own business, when out of a clear blue sky comes this gunboat, telling him that El Jefe wants to talk to him at headquarters back on Laputa. And they won't even say what they want to talk to him about. What's the story?"

"Well, the sky out there is black, and the NAUSS *Ciudad Juárez* is a light cruiser, not a gunboat. And the place where Cantrell is, Mundito Rosinante, was built as a joint project between the Panablancos' Scadiwa and the Japanese Mitsui. We found massive files of correspondence between Cantrell and the Panoblancos, and while he himself does not appear to be in any sort of trouble, we would like to talk to him about some of the people he knows. He has had dealings with Llamamoto of the Tellurbank, for instance. And his opinions of any number of third parties would be very helpful to Security."

"And you couldn't send a man to interview him?"

"Actually, we invited him to come to Laputa, and he refused to come. The initial contact seems to have been made by a computer in one of our field offices, and we may have got off on the wrong foot at the beginning."

"It sounds like it to me, Mr. Hulvey. However, it is my understanding that the P.O. on the *Juárez* wants to bring Cantrell back to Laputa to face unspecified charges. Senator Gomez wants to know what those charges are."

"I'll look into the matter and get back to you," Hulvey said. "I'm sneaking out this call from a teleconference, but I'll look into the matter for you."

"Look into the matter for the Senator, too," said Maria Yellowknife. "Adios, Señor Deputy Administrator Hulvey."

"What a bitch," Hulvey said sourly. The teleconference was now talking about the Mexican Revolution in 1915.

"The Regional Administrators seem very knowledgeable about names and dates and places," said Corporate Elna. "In fact, I suspect that most of them are hiding behind their telecon screens the same way you are, and letting their ushabtis do the talking for them on nonsubstantive matters."

"You could be right. Okay, put me on again."

"Paul Muni gave a better performance as Benito Juárez than Marlon Brando did as Emiliano Zapata," said one.

"Did you know that Benito Mussolini was named after Benito Juárez?" said another.

"That's mildly interesting," said Hulvey. "However,

we seem to be running over our set time. I would like to suggest that we adjourn until our next weekly meeting." A ripple passed across the faces displayed on his telecon screen as the simulated Regional Administrators came to life and then agreed to adjourn.

"So Holt has located Corporate Susan Brown, has he?" Hulvey mused. "Then tell Major Terry that we will *not* specify the charges against Cantrell. Stall it a day or two. We can find out from Holt what's likely to happen."

"What about Senator Gomez?"

"I'll have to write that letter myself, I guess. It'll be pure bullshit, but as a senator he's entitled to the best."

CHAPTER 5

Lieutenant Holt put on the light blue guayabera he had picked up at the local store, and hung the square-cut shirttail of the four-pocket, short-sleeved shirt outside his crisply pressed khaki trousers. He checked his shoeshine, looked himself over in the full-length mirror on back of his cabin door, and strolled down the corridor to the communications room of the NAUSS *Ciudad Juárez* carrying his attaché case.

Inside, a petty officer was reading the daily news dispatches posted on the bulletin board, a rating was filing a report, and the communications officer, a lieutenant ten years Holt's junior, was playing solitaire. Holt walked over to the desk, and when the lieutenant didn't look up, he reached over and played a red seven on a black eight. The man looked up from his game.

"Hello, Holt. You want to use the encoding booth again?" He looked around. "It's open, go ahead."

"Much grass, John," Holt said, and walked over to the booth. He sat down, closed the door, and took his encryption key from his case. Putting the key in its slot, he set the mode for voice and hit the On button. A yellow light came on that said ENCODING.

FROM: LT. O.J. HOLT; SUBJECT: STATUS REPORT UPDATE; TO: DEPUTY ADMINISTRATOR WILLIAM M. HULVEY; DATE: 4 MAR 41, 2110 HOURS.

WILLY, I HAVEN'T BEEN ABLE TO GET ANYTHING OUT OF CORPORATE SUSIE. ALL THE NICE, FRIENDLY INTERVIEWS IN THE WORLD WON'T SHAKE ANYTHING LOOSE FROM HER, AND IN THE CIRCUMSTANCES I CAN'T HARDLY THREATEN TO TAKE HER APART, IF *that* WOULD DO ANY GOOD. OKAY. MAJOR TERRY DIDN'T SIGN MY REQUISITION FOR PLASTIQUE BACK ON LAPUTA I JUST FOUND OUT, BECAUSE HE COULDN'T IMAGINE WHAT I'D USE IT FOR. NEVER THOUGHT I'D BE MISSING GREENE, BUT THE OLD FART HAD HIS USES. ANYWAY, I HAVE BEEN COORDINATING WITH TERRY PRETTY CLOSELY, AND HE HAS SET UP THE MARINES TO RAID CANTRELL'S HEADQUARTERS TONIGHT AT 0200, THAT IS, 5 MARCH 41 AT 0200 IS THE TIME. TONIGHT IS THE NIGHT. I THINK HIS PLAN LEAVES A LOT TO BE DESIRED, FRANKLY, AND CANTRELL MOVES AROUND A LOT, TOO, SO IF HE MISSES, THERE ISN'T GOING TO BE ANOTHER SHOT AT CORPORATE SUSIE FOR A GOOD LONG TIME. SO I'M GOING OUT WITH THE PROVERBIAL FIELD EXPEDIENT. PLASTIQUE WOULD BE BETTER, BUT YOU TAKE WHAT YOU CAN GET. THIS WILL BE A SOMEWHAT BIGGER CHARGE THAN I WOULD PREFER TO USE, NOT AS NEATLY PLACED. IF TERRY PULLS IT OFF, I CAN STILL SIFT THROUGH THE RUBBLE FOR PIECES OF VON ZWANG'S NOTEBOOK. IF TERRY BLOWS IT, WHICH I THINK IS MORE LIKELY, NOBODY IS GOING TO NOTICE ONE MORE EXPLOSION, AND WE MAY NEVER FIND OUT IF OLD SUSIE HAD THE NOTEBOOK.

I'M REAL PLEASED TO HEAR THAT DAN GRADUATED

FIRST IN HIS CLASS AT MISSILE SCHOOL. GIVE HIM MY
REGARDS THE NEXT TIME YOU SEE HIM.

SO LONG, OLD BUDDY.

"How do you want the message signed?" asked the
machine.

"Oh, sign it 'Buck,' I guess," said Holt. He read over
his message and pushed the Send button. Beside the
yellow light that said ENCODING, a red light went on that
said SENDING. The two lights went off together, and he
put his encryption key back in the attaché case and
sauntered off.

The NAUSS *Ciudad Juárez* is built like a wheel with
three spokes around a hub containing the power plant,
weapons systems, and magazines. The ship rotates to
provide its crew on the rim with centrifugal force, and,
of course, when the ship docks at another rotating object, it is first necessary to match velocities, and second
to match rotations. Once velocity and rotation match,
ship and station are carefully brought together, their
airlocks open in an embrace, and the seals tumesce to
keep both systems airtight. Geometrically, it is difficult
to put the ship's airlock anyplace except on one end of
the hub, normally at the end of the axis of rotation.

Holt took an elevator into the hub, where, instead of
going through the open airlock, he went into the minor
magazine—not the missile-storage, but the small-arms
room. The door, like all the magazine doors, was
guarded by a Cerberus Security Computer. Holt's connection with Security, however, had afforded him access to the sop bucket, and he entered as softly as any
shadow. Once inside, he selected the smallest available
demolition charge, a tiny nuclear warhead yielding the
equivalent of fifteen tons of TNT, with its chemical explosive detonator. He opened his attaché case and removed a small wheeled luggage carrier and a cloth
AWOL bag. He removed the warhead from the demolition charge, put it in his attaché case under a folded
windbreaker, and slipped the AWOL bag over the demolition charge. He then strapped the thinly disguised

bomb onto the luggage carrier, closed his attaché case, and walked out. Trailing nearly twenty kilograms of high explosive behind him on the little carrier, and carrying the equivalent of 15,000 kilograms of high explosive in his left hand, he sauntered down to the airlock to go out on the town. The marines checked his pass to make sure it was in order, and the militia that was there to stop the marines paid no attention to him. He walked past the militia checkpoint below the airlock, and past the militia company set up at the Express Elevator Transfer Station, without more than a perfunctory challenge. Then came the long elevator ride to the Drop Ship Station.

The physical layout of Mundito Rosinante is this: two counterrotating cylinders, seven kilometers in diameter, fifty kilometers long, the axes of rotation pointed at the sun. The mainframe, at the inner cap, holds the cylinders 125 kilometers apart, center to center, and the whole is set in an immense field of mirrors, which can be individually controlled to produce remarkable effects. The Drop Ship is the most expeditious manner of moving from one cylinder to the other, and since the ship was docked on the right-hand cylinder, and Corporate Susan Brown was situated in the left-hand cylinder, Lieutenant Holt sat with his bomb in the Drop Ship Station and waited for the Drop Ship to arrive.

When it came, he boarded with perhaps a score of other passengers. Wishing to avoid notice, he studiously avoided noticing them. The Drop Ship, once the passengers were aboard, rode out on a track to a point on the outer skin of the cylinder, and at a precisely timed instant it released its magnetic grapples. On board, one gee dropped to zero as the ship was thrown from the right-hand cylinder with a tangential velocity of 262 meters per second, to cross the distance between the two Drop Ship Stations in 478 seconds of free-fall. The Drop Ship computer counted the trip down, at ten-second intervals until the last ten seconds, which were done individually. At the count of ". . . two, one, zero!" the magnetic grapples locked onto the Drop Ship Station on the other side, and everybody laughed. The passengers disembarked, and Holt walked out of the Station. The air was much cooler here. Holt opened his attaché case and removed his windbreaker. He unfolded it, turned the aluminum side in and the brown side out, and slipped it on. Then, closing the case, he headed up the hill that was mounded on top of the Station. The grass had been mowed that day, and the evening air smelled green and sweet beside the kempt hedges. Holt walked along with his bomb, unchallenged. The house at the top of the hill was where Corporate Susan Brown was established.

There was a light in the window. That was unexpected and unwelcome. Holt slipped up to the building and, being careful to make no sound, looked inside. A young militiaman was reading at a desk. Evidently something Holt had said had made Corporate Susie nervous. Holt smiled faintly; perhaps she didn't like his looks. He shrugged. It was too bad about the guard. Toting his bomb, he went very quietly around to the back. The door was locked, but he took a plastic card, a joker, from his guayabera pocket and opened it. He left the explosive and carrier by the door and walked into the lit room, carrying his attaché case.

"Hey, Sam," he said, walking up, "I have something for you."

"My name is Rudy," said the guard, pushing himself away from the table.

Holt hit him a killing blow with the edge of his right hand and laid the body out of sight of the monitors. The first time they checked, they might assume that Rudy had gone to the bathroom.

He went back and got the explosive. He unstrapped it, and went down the hall toward the room where Corporate Susan Brown's memory banks were stored, the explosive in his right hand, balanced by the attaché case in his left. He was wondering whether or not he should change the 0200-hour setting on the time, because it was only 2345. On the one hand, the explosive might be discovered because of that fool guard; on the other, Major Terry's surprise attack on Cantrell's headquarters might be jeopardized. He never came to any decision; as he stepped around the corner, a burst of microwave radiation detonated the explosive device he was carrying.

Thus died Joe Bob Baroody of the Contra Darwin, also known as Lieutenant Oscar James Holt of the Military Intelligence Service.

CHAPTER 6

Lieutenant Holt's Status Report Update of 4 March 41/2110 was sitting on Hulvey's desk when the Deputy Administrator arrived at his office on the morning of the fifth. He put it on the decoding tray and told Corporate Elna which encryption key to use. The codes involved were highly sophisticated, and de facto unbreakable, but the name of the key was NIWRAD ARTNOC, Contra Darwin spelled backward. His desk pushed up the hard copy to him and he read it through quickly.

"Where's the latest update?" he asked.

"That is the latest update," Corporate Elna replied. "There is no later word from Rosinante."

"Well, whatever was going to happen is history by now," Hulvey said. "Ask for a current Status Report. Not an update, a full report."

"Do you want Holt to report?" asked the computer. "If you want Major Terry, we have to go NAVY-Security via NAUGA-Navy. If you want Captain Lowell, we have to go NAVY-Operations via NAUGA-Navy."

"Of course I want Holt to report! Christ! He should have reported hours ago. I want to know what the hell is going on."

"I will try to contact Lieutenant Holt directly," Corporate Elna said, "and I will also request a current Status Report on the NAUSS *Ciudad Juárez* from NAUGA-Navy. Concurrently, simultaneously, and immediately."

"Good." Hulvey nodded. "When will you have it?"

"When we get it. NAUGA-Navy may have the report already in hand, or it may have to be prepared in the field. Since there is a forty-five-minute lag while light makes a round trip, you should have something before noon at the latest."

"I wonder if something happened?" said Hulvey.

"Yes," said Corporate Elna. "NAUGA-Navy informs me that the NAUSS *Ciudad Juárez* discontinued communication at 0209:35 this morning, and has not responded to requests to resume communication."

"Oh?" said Hulvey. He walked over to the Imperial Russian Samovar, certified to have belonged to a Tsarist general, and drew himself a cup of tea. "That doesn't sound too good, now, does it?"

"Would you like some cherry preserves for your tea? We have some little plastic containers in the sugar drawer."

"No, thank you," he said, carefully sipping the scalding tea from his styrofoam cup. The phone rang.

"Administrator Bowman has been called before today's meeting with the Senate Committee on Internal Security," said Corporate Elna. "He wants to know what has been done about the wave of bombings in Regions 7 and 9."

"Two bombings don't make a wave," said Hulvey, "even bombings of Federal buildings. Should I take it from the telecon seat?"

"Mr. Bowman would prefer that you do so," the computer said. Hulvey looked at the clock. It was still a quarter of an hour before his official starting time. The phone rang.

"Maria Yellowknife from Senator Gomez's office," said Corporate Elna.

Hulvey walked over to the telecon seat with his steaming teacup. "Find out what she wants, and tell her I'm briefing the Administrator for an appearance before the Senate," he said.

After the briefing, Hulvey held a meeting with the head of his Program Control and Evaluation Division. They discussed the various ants in the amber of NAUGA-Security's gemlike organization. Then he took over a group of visiting firemen—security officials from France, Belgium, Scotland, Spain, and Portugal—that Bowman was to have met with. Hulvey gave them the tour and went to lunch with them.

When he returned to his office, Corporate Elna had a stack of priority items for his attention. He drew himself a cup of tea from the samovar and waded into them. The last item was a copy of a short memorandum sent over from NAUGA-Navy.

Date: 5 March 41
From: Governor's Office, Mundito Rosinante
Subj: NAUSS *Ciudad Juárez*, Status Report
To: NAUGA-Navy; Attn: Operations (VTG)

This is in reply to your 5 March 41 request for information on the current status of the NAUSS *Ciudad Juárez*.

Following a covert and unprovoked attempt to destroy the Prenatal Care Clinic with a nuclear device, the Rosinante Militia seized control of the NAUSS *Ciudad Juárez* at about 0215 hours today.

Casualty lists are being prepared and will be forwarded when available. Preliminary estimates are 15 dead, all marines except one, 28 wounded and 2 missing, all marines.

/s/
Marian Yashon for CCCantrell

Hulvey called in Dolores Ferranes and showed her the memo.

"Well, well, Mr. Hulvey, sir," she said, handing the hard copy back to him. Then she plugged in her cobra and rolled herself a cigarette. She struck a kitchen match with her thumbnail and lit up. "I suppose it wouldn't be too helpful to tell you that the shit has hit the fan?"

"No," said Hulvey, "I was able to figure that out myself. How do we limit the damage?"

"First we find out what the damage is," she said, exhaling smoke. "Did they merely find the bomb in place and jump the ship? If so, they might not be able to tie it to Holt at all."

"That would be nice," said Hulvey. "What if they caught Holt red-handed?"

"That wouldn't be so nice," Ferranes agreed. "Even so, the locals probably wouldn't follow the worst line of questioning. If he goes back to Laputa, though, he'll be too hot to help out."

"We can burn that bridge after we cross it," he said. "Holt may not even be alive." Ferranes blew a smoke ring and watched it for a moment.

"Maybe not," she said at last. "I expect we'll find out in a day or two." She flicked ash at the cobra. "We can't do anything until we know what the score is. Except you *will* have to talk to Bowman."

"Right. I'll tell him what we have. As soon as I can get hold of him. Hey, Elna?"

"Yes, sir?"

"Plug me in for ten minutes with the Administrator asap."

"He's in his limousine on the way back from the Senate. Should I cut in on his conversation?"

"No, I don't want to panic him. Make that appointment at his earliest possible convenience. And stay in touch with NAUGA-Navy. We can let them front for us in talking to Cantrell, at least for now."

That night Hulvey dreamed of a little girl in a print

dress who ran from him crying: "Don't hurt Jennie! Don't hurt Jennie!"

7 March '41
Evening

Dear Riordan,

This letter is encoded for read only, no hard copy. I urge you to honor that request.

We keep forgetting that we are mortal. We know it, but we disremember, and then—what a shock!— a friend dies, and in the grief for his death we anticipate our own.

Joe Bob once asked me: "Why aren't you right with God anymore?" The best answer I could ever find was that in seeking to do God's work, I had somehow transgressed on God's laws, and so fallen from grace. It is, I suppose, a bit like dying for your country: one does it in a fit of enthusiasm, and is never the same afterward.

I have received word from Rosinante that Joe Bob Baroody is dead. He died doing God's work, but he was one of those lucky men who never doubted his actions. I know he died in a state of grace.

A little before midnight on 4 March, Joe Bob was killed when a device he was carrying into the Prenatal Care Clinic exploded prematurely. The clinic in question is operated by Corporate Susan Brown. For what it is worth, I am now utterly positive that she has the von Zwang notebook.

The Rosinante Militia—surely something out of a comic opera—used that explosion, if they did not cause it, as the pretext to launch an attack on the *Juárez*. Incredibly, they were able to take the ship. It would appear that Major Terry had dispatched marines to seize Cantrell, so that the ship lay open and undefended. If Major Terry was guilty of an error of judgment, he paid the full price for it.

The authorities on Rosinante claimed that the device that killed Holt was nuclear, and as Holt's superior officer, Terry was tried on charges of terrorism with a nuclear device. Under NAU law, the charge carries a mandatory death penalty, and they sent Terry up before a tin-can judge, with Corporate Susan Brown as the tin-can prosecutor. Needless to say, Terry was found guilty and promptly shot full of heroin. That was pretty rough, but things are going to get worse.

The way things stand right now, the Rosinante Militia has pulled the whole Political Section, computers, informers, and all, off the *Juárez*. For interrogation, they say. And the ship was sent back home. The situation is that Rosinante is holding *our* people, while the Navy blames *us* for the dead marines. Stanley Bowman is very upset over this. And very worried. I sat up with him as he killed a liter of bourbon. I finally poured him into bed and went home.

He is right to worry. It is only a matter of time before Holt is identified as Baroody, and the Contra Darwin is tied to Security. I had planned to get you on the President's Security Force. It is the fastest of fast tracks, and you would have made Rear Admiral before you were thirty. No more. As a line officer you will be much better placed to survive my fall, and in the natural course of events you will shortly go aboard the NAUSS *Vancouver* as the Chief Political Officer.

At work I will hold firm, shoring up poor old Bowman and defending myself with vigor, but at night, talking to you, Riordan, I confess I am in despair. I remain, your father.

/s/

William Hulvey

Commander Riordan Hulvey sat watching the luminous screen. Presently it blinked three times, very slowly, and went out.

Hulvey stormed into the Administrator's suite of offices.

"What the hell is going on?" he said. Dolores Ferranes, her blouse ripped off one shoulder, was trying to roll a cigarette and spilling most of the tobacco on the textured Oriental carpet. Administrator Stanley Bowman was lying face down on the Louis Quinze sofa, weeping. Great racking sobs shook his body.

"Stanley called me in and propositioned me in the crudest manner imaginable," she said, "and when I put him off, he got physical and lunged at me. I used aikido and threw him, and when he started to get up I told him: 'That's no way to treat a coconspirator!' He just collapsed on the couch and started to cry."

"Oh, for God's sake." Hulvey walked over to the medallion cabinet, a commissioned copy of an original in the Gulbkenian collection, and opened it. Inside were two 750-ml bottles of bourbon, both nearly empty. He poured out a short shot and dropped the bottles in the wastebasket.

"Bowman, you asshole!" he thundered. "Sit up and stop that blubbering!" When the sobbing subsided, Hulvey said: "Sit up and drink this." The Administrator sat up, and Hulvey handed him the drink, which he tossed off.

"Now then, what the hell is going on?" Hulvey asked.

"Can I have another drink?" said Bowman. He started to hiccup.

"That's all there was, Stan. Now what's the trouble?"

Bowman didn't answer, he just put his face in his hands and hiccuped. Hulvey took the shot glass and filled it with water from the sterling-silver carafe on the sideboy, another Gulbkenian strikeoff.

"Hey, Stan," he said, "you hear me?" Bowman nodded, hiccuping. "Fine, now exhale. You know, breathe out all the way and hold it." Bowman exhaled, hiccuping, and Hulvey handed him the glass of water. "Drink this without breathing in," he said. Bowman drank about half the water, and finally inhaled with a great sigh. He gave the glass back to Hulvey.

"Okay, Stan. You want to tell me about it? Why were you bawling like a stuck calf just now?"

"I was up for a Senate Committee meeting today," Bowman said after a pause. "The Budget Committee. Senator Gomez of Texas came in about halfway through." He stopped for a moment. "It's been a long time since we got burned on Rosinante, you know? Weeks. And I've been worried all that time that they were going to turn up. . . ." He stopped, then took hold of himself. "Turn up the connection between Lieutenant Holt and Joe Bob Baroody. Joe Bob used to be one of my aides in the Creationist Coalition, you know, back in the old days." He sighed. "It never happened, you know?"

"Yeah, Stan," Hulvey nodded, "I've been watching that myself."

"Right. So I decided, Hey, maybe we going to luck out on this. Maybe we can just bury our dead and go on. And then this afternoon, this after—noon . . ." Bowman's eyes filled with tears, and the corners of his mouth turned sharply down. Hulvey grabbed him by the shoulders and shook him violently, dislodging Bowman's rimless glasses.

"You're right, Willy," said Bowman. He put his glasses back on, and then took them off to wipe his eyes with his handkerchief. Finally he blew his nose.

"Could I have another drink, Willy, please?" he asked. "I badly need a drink."

"You're fresh out," Hulvey said, "unless you want water. Go on."

"Yeah. This afternoon Gomez walked in and did a number on me about Governor Panoblanco. Hell, that's ancient history. They never found a thing that wasn't circumstantial, and with Greene dead, we're clean as a whistle."

"Go on," said Hulvey.

"Then he asked me if I knew that Holt was Baroody. Not in those words, exactly, but he knew enough to tie the can to my tail. I denied everything, of course, but Willy, I was lying under oath! I was perjuring myself! And they can prove it!"

"Do you have the transcript of the conversation?" Ferranes asked.

"It's on my desk," Bowman said. "I was reading it when I asked you in. I wanted to ask you something."

Hulvey and Ferranes picked up the transcript of the committee meeting, highlighted where Senator Gomez took over, and read through the critical parts.

"You handled yourself real well, Stan," Hulvey said. "This here's a good job."

"You do have a problem, however," Ferranes added. "If Gomez is out to get you, perjury is the least of your troubles."

"They can't prove I did anything," protested Bowman, "but they can prove I committed perjury and force my resignation. I could go to jail for perjury!"

"Hey, Stan," Ferranes sat down beside him and took his hand, "forget about the perjury, okay? Holt died carrying a nuclear device, trying to commit what the court called an act of terrorism. The next guy in the chain of command was that poor mutt Terry. He was put to sleep after a trial by a NAU judge, in a NAU court, under NAU law. Gomez is trying to hang a rap of nuclear terrorism on you."

"But why does he care about Rosinante?" Bowman asked plaintively.

"Cantrell is one of his constituents," said Hulvey sourly. "For Christ's sake, Bowman! He *knows* you killed Panoblanco with that goddamn cruise missile, but he can't prove it, okay? He *can* prove the connection with Holt, and as far as Gomez is concerned, that's just as good."

"Then let's get Gomez!" Bowman showed a flash of his old spirit. "First," he added.

"Hey, Stan," said Hulvey very gently, "in case you hadn't noticed, things are pretty tense with the Hispanics right now. Gomez is the leader of the very small group of Hispanic senators who aren't antihegemonists. If he dies, it could be the spark that touches off a civil war."

"You're so smart, you do something about Senator

Gomez," said Bowman. "Your ass is in the crack too, you know."

"That's true," Hulvey agreed. "I'll have Schlecter give him a call. Maybe we can cut a deal."

Ferranes motioned him to one side. "Gomez won't deal," she said softly. "If he wanted to deal, he would have come around with what he had."

"It can't hurt to ask," Hulvey said. "And just because a man doesn't *want* to deal, doesn't mean that he won't."

"Mr. Hulvey," Ferranes said, "Senator Gomez is out for blood. Bowman's blood, your blood. When he gets around to mopping up, maybe even mine. Sure, he wants to keep the North American Union whole, but he also wants to avenge the murder of Governor Panoblanco. He will not cut a deal."

"If Gomez dies, that means secession and probably civil war," said Hulvey. "Of course, there isn't any guarantee that that won't happen if he stays alive."

"You know the flip side of that coin?" she asked.

"What do you mean?"

"If Gomez stays alive, we're in serious trouble," Ferranes said. "If he dies, there isn't any guarantee that we'll get out." She snuffed out her cigarette on the sole of her shoe and dropped it into a cobalt-blue Sevres porcelain vase with gilt bronze trim.

CHAPTER 7

John Gomez, the senior Senator from Texas, sat in his office with his legislative and administrative assistants, Maria Yellowknife and Alan Watkins.

"You really should go to Abilene," said Watkins.

"It's a two-bit rubber-chicken fund raiser, but most of the antihegemonistas that might swing to you are going to be there."

"It's the key to the caucus in Houston," said Maria. "If you can split them, the antihegemonists probably won't put a candidate up against you in next year's primary."

"I'd win hands down," Gomez said. "But it's so much nicer to run unopposed. Okay, put Abilene on my schedule. Did I tell you Bob Schlecter called this morning?" He smiled, stroking his mustache with his forefinger.

"No," said Watkins. Maria shook her head.

"He wants me to lay off Bowman in Security. The President needs Bowman, he said. We couldn't get a new head of Security through the Senate, he said. We might even unblock the funds for the Central Texas Agricultural Desalinated Water Authority, he said."

"Where have I heard that one before?" asked Maria.

"Schlecter said most of the senior staff in Security would resign if Bowman was forced out." He laughed. "I said, who'd miss 'em? He had to admit nobody would, but Security would be dead in the water at a real bad time. The bottom line was, would I please lay off good old Stanley Bowman?"

"You aren't going to let that murdering son of a bitch off the hook, are you?" asked Watkins.

"Oh, hell no," replied Gomez. "But Schlecter wanted to do me something to show he was sincere, so I said why don't you turn loose B.J. Coya? He hemmed and hawed, but old B.J. called about an hour ago to thank me for getting him out of jail."

"Big deal," said Watkins.

"He's still in the Texas House of Delegates, even if he isn't Speaker anymore," said Maria. "He still knows everybody, and he is a number-one smooth operator. He could help at Houston."

"Sure," said Gomez. "I won't need his help in Houston, but in the election he could do me some good."

"Maybe fifty thousand votes," said Watkins. "He

led you by more than sixty thousand in his district last time."

"Hey," said Maria, "if Schlecter is sincere, what happens when you don't lay off Bowman?"

"That's a good question," said Gomez. "The Administration won't do anything—I'm too valuable as their pet antihegemonista Hispanic, but between the time Bowman realizes he's hit, and the time he's down, he or his pistolero Hulvey might do something." He shrugged. "I choose to accept the risk. It is something a man must do." He smiled, showing his gold bicuspid. "I have, however, been working on a contingency plan with Corporate Zapata."

"What contingency, Chief?" asked Maria, very softly.

"Hah! It's sort of like those sealed letters in the old gangster movies, the ones that get sent to the D.A. by an anonymous friend," he said. "The only difference is, I don't expect to know what hits me. So the reason for the—call it a sealed letter if you like—is not to threaten my enemies, but to avenge myself upon them. I've been working on it for a while, and I must say the doing of it has cheered me considerably."

"Don't let your sense of humor get you in trouble," cautioned Watkins, seriously.

"Hey, Alan," Gomez grinned and punched him lightly on the arm, "this is for when I'm dead!" He laughed. "Some of that stuff I'd never say if I thought I'd hear the end of it!"

Commander David Riordan Hulvey, Senior Political Officer of the NAUSS *Vancouver*, sat in the galley of the officers' mess with a piece of Dutch apple pie and a cup of coffee.

"The difference between apple pie and Dutch apple pie?" said the cook. "Dutch apple pie is made with schnitz instead of apples."

"What's schnitz?" asked Riordan.

"Schnitz is dried apples. Not freeze-dried, or processed, but air-dried. So they're kind of chewy. Weight for weight, schnitz is sweeter than apples, so the pie is sweeter, too."

"It's good pie," said Riordan. "Why don't they call it schnitz pie?" His belt phone rang, and he snapped it open.

"You wished to be kept informed about Senator Gomez," said the Security computer. It would have qualified for incorporation, had it not been wholly owned by NAUGA-Security. "The twenty-four-hour news station KSLN just broadcast the report that Senator Gomez died in a plane crash at Abilene, Texas." It hesitated. "There is an unusual aspect to the report."

"Go on," said Riordan.

"The report appears to be in the form of Senator Gomez holding a posthumous press conference, sir."

"What!? I want transcripts! How far have they gone? Tune me in on it!"

Riordan sat in the galley listening to the reporters at the press conference asking questions of Corporate Zapata, the Senator's personal computer.

In order to anticipate the questions that Senator Gomez might be asked, Corporate Zapata had compiled individual paradigms for each reporter in the St. Louis press corps. Senator Gomez then gave as the situation his press conference after his political assassination, and answered the questions put forward by Corporate Zapata—using the paradigms—on behalf of the various reporters. The answers were taped and stored, and when a live reporter asked an anticipated question, Corporate Zapata played the prerecorded answer. The late Senator Gomez was advocating secession and treason in a calm, reasonable, and devastating manner, spiced with his country wit.

"Put me through to NAUGA-Security in St. Louis," Riordan said. "I want the Deputy Administrator." He could have called his father directly, but he wanted to be on record as going through channels. By the time he had eaten his pie, the call had gone through. He told his father what was going on, and his father, after listening to a question or two, excused himself. About the end of Riordan's second cup of coffee the press conference ended.

"This here killing of Chicano politicians has just naturally got to stop," said the recorded voice of Senator Gomez, and the Security police walked into the Senator's office where the press conference was being held and very politely terminated the broadcast.

"Hey," said Riordan, "Dad made real good time on that." He finished his coffee.

"Another cup, sir?" asked the cook.

"No," replied Riordan, "I have work to do."

He went down to the communications center and put the NAUSS *Vancouver* on yellow alert. Specifically, he ordered the Security Forces on ship to be prepared to deal with a mutiny in the next twenty-four hours. Then he went down to the missile bay and, after identifying himself to the guard, sat down at the minor terminal.

"Good morning, 1848," he said. The words floated up on the display screen as the terminal converted speech to print. Missile 1848 could handle print. It had no speech capability. "Have your modifications been completed?"

YES, COMMANDER HULVEY, floated up on the screen. The terminal would have provided speech output if asked, but Riordan, not being illiterate, didn't feel the need for simultaneous translation. "The GMB Mark II has been replaced with a GMB Mark IC4, configured for maximum range. It is installed and properly seated."

"Very good, 1848. I am now going to give you the terminal ballistic description to go with the course information you already have. Are you ready to receive?"

AFFIRMATIVE. Riordan then keyed in the Security computer, which read off the complete file on Mundito Rosinante, including the last known position of Corporate Susan Brown.

THANK YOU FOR TARGET INFORMATION. IS PRESENT WARHEAD SATISFACTORY?

"What is the yield of your present warhead?"

NOMINAL YIELD OF WARHEAD #412487.42 IS ONE
MEGATON. THE WARHEAD, HOWEVER, IS 9 YEARS, 4
MONTHS OLD AND WILL PROBABLY YIELD NO MORE
THAN 96 PERCENT NOMINAL VALUE WITH NORMAL
DETONATION PROTOCOL.

"That appears to be entirely satisfactory," said Riordan. "Maintain readiness to launch for twenty-four
hours."

THIS MISSILE IS GRATIFIED TO BE OF USE.

Captain Robert Lowell, of the NAUSS *Ciudad
Juárez*, was rejoining the L-4 Fleet when he heard the
posthumous press conference. Not the original broadcast, but the rebroadcast by JapaNews two hours later.

Lowell had several problems. He was facing a court-
martial for the loss of his ship to the Rosinante Militia.
The defense that the PO, Major Terry, had assumed
command of the ship at the time would be a mitigating
circumstance at best. He had lost his ship in a combat
situation, and even if he escaped going to the stockade,
his career was a shambles. Also, when the authorities
on Rosinante returned his ship to his command, they
had pulled off the Political Section, which, by no coin-
cidence, overlapped and included the Security Section.
Consequently, the crew had discovered that they were
either for Mexico Libre or a restoration of the Old Regime, or, since the two were not incompatible, both of
them. The final consideration was internal. Captain
Lowell was profoundly alienated from the North American Union Government that he served. His sympathies
lay with the Old Regime, yet he was political realist
enough to understand that the Old Regime was dead beyond any hope of resuscitation. Equally, he sympa-
thized with the political aspirations of the crew, but
could conceive of no useful action that could be taken.
The long voyage home had been a very bad time for
him. His frustration led him to introspection, and his
introspection increased his frustration. Without knowing what he wanted, he wanted very badly to act.

Senator Gomez's posthumous press conference was

the seed that crystallized his decision. It was the sign he had been waiting for, and his action was heartfelt, spontaneous, and immediate. The NAUSS *Ciudad Juárez* moved into the L-4 Fleet broadcasting the forbidden anthem of the Old Regime, "The Star-Spangled Banner," and "Guantanamera," the song from Mexico's bloody history that had been adopted by the Hispanic Nationalists.

There were speeches also, but they were hardly needed. The late Senator Gomez and the music were enough to orchestrate the uprisings that swept through the fleet.

These uprisings were not uniformly successful. Here and there, Security maintained control, as a few Political Officers, luckier or more astute than their fellows, performed as they were intended to. Bitter fighting on board ship was the rule where the NAU retained control, and the mutinous ships moved swiftly to the aid of their fellows.

The bad news rolled into the office of Deputy Administrator William Hulvey, building from one crescendo to the next. Humans and computers labored to keep the situation boards up to date. Orders, disconnected from reality, went out to Political Officers held captive or dead. Orders, seeking to contain the catastrophe, pushed desperately at string.

Hulvey sat back, watching chaos swirl around him, engulfing not him alone, but NAUGA-Security, NAUGA-Navy, the Executive Office, the NAU itself. They didn't know it yet, perhaps, but they would find out very soon. Maybe Navy already knew.

"Where the bloody hell is Bowman?" he asked resignedly. The Administrator couldn't help, but it might be some comfort to have him standing by.

"He was called to the Executive Mansion a few minutes before all this started up," said Corporate Elna. "Schlecter said the President was very upset at Senator Gomez's death. The Administrator made a joke about being shot, and Schlecter didn't think it was funny at all."

"I don't think it's funny, either," said Hulvey. He walked over to the samovar and drew himself a cup of tea, adding a plastic cuplet of cherry preserves. "Try and get him on the horn, anyway. He ought to know about this immediately." He went back to his desk and sat down.

"Yes, sir," said Corporate Elna. "You have a message from the P.O. of the L-5 Fleet, and from your son." The message from Rear Admiral Hildebrand contained the kernel of news that the senior officers of the L-5 Fleet were caucussing to decide what to do about the mutiny in the L-4 Fleet. The husk surrounding that kernel was an elaborate justification of Hildebrand's actions and inactions and a wholesale placing of blame on his subordinates. The message from Commander David Riordan Hulvey said simply: "Dear Father, I have assumed command of the NAUSS *Vancouver*. God's will be done. Long live the North American Union!"

Hulvey sat back wearily, and felt the back of his neck and shoulders being massaged. "Hey, Dolores, didn't the shit hit the fan *this* time?"

"It sure did, Willy. You're going to need a bulldozer to clean it all up."

Hulvey stirred the cherry preserves in his cup and took a sip. "And here I sit with a fucking teaspoon."

CHAPTER 8

Commander David Riordan Hulvey walked into the conning room of the NAUSS *Vancouver*, printing blood on the deck with his left foot.

"Engine room report," he said, "do we have power for the main drive?"

"Negatori," was the staticky response, "the mutineers (inaudible) the reactor (inaudible) gauges smashed. Probably take a few days (inaudible) emergency repairs. We could maybe jury-rig something (inaudible) going soonest."

"We need to get underway as fast as possible," said Riordan. "Do what you have to do, but for God's sake, get us moving!" He looked at the big situation screen. The NAUSS *Vancouver* had established a battle plane, with the *Seattle*—the *Vancouver*'s sister ship—and the *Artur Rubinstein*, a forty-year-old cruiser serving as a training ship, as the other two points of the plane. The *Seattle* was 982 kilometers and closing. In about half an hour, the *Seattle* would be near enough to float over marines.

"Mr. Lincoln," he said, "have we made any progress retaking the number-one airlock?"

"Negatori," came the swift reply, "we threw in our last reserves to retake the engine room." The situation screen showed a new ship approaching, below the plane of battle by 23 degrees, and 170 degrees away from the *Seattle*. As Riordan watched, the distance was registered at 2575 kilometers, and the ship was identified as the NAUSS *Wyoming*.

"Are we in contact with the *Seattle*?" he asked.

"Yes, sir," said the communications computer.

"Get me direct voice communication with the captain, if you can."

"Yes, sir," said the computer, then, "You can use your belt phone, sir, you're patched through Lambda-1 in the L-4's."

Riordan snapped open his phone. There was background noise rather than a dial tone. "Ahoy! Am I talking to the captain of the NAUSS *Seattle*?"

"I seem to be the captain," said a pleasant voice, "and this is the *Seattle*, all right, but we haven't settled on the initials, yet. What can we do for you?"

"Stop closing."

"Sorry, *Vancouver*, we've spilled too much blood to back off now." A pause, with side conversation. "Martinez says: 'Surrender or die.' "

"Doesn't he mean 'Surrender *and* die'?" asked Riordan.

"Modern communications are *such* a pain," said the pleasant voice. "Look, are you Commander Hulvey?"

"I am he."

"Well, then, I'll give you my personal word of honor, Commander, that if you surrender, you won't be harmed."

"It's always a pleasure to meet a man with a personal word of honor, but I fear you have the advantage on me."

"In more ways than one," said the pleasant voice. "I'm Staff Sergeant Burton Smith, formerly on the power-supply detail."

"Well, then, Captain Smith, I need some time to talk matters over with my officers. If you will stop closing, I will get back to you in half an hour. *Hasta la vista*."

"*Adios*, Commander Hulvey," said Smith, "I'll see what I can do."

The situation screen showed the *Seattle* still closing.

"Gunnery," said Riordan, "target three missiles on

the *Seattle*, and target one to start for the *Seattle* and hook over to the *Rubinstein* at the last possible moment."

"Missiles targeted," said a woman's voice.

"Load and prepare to fire on command," said Riordan. "Further missiles are to be targeted on the *Seattle* except as otherwise noted." He looked at the situation screen. The *Seattle* was 722 kilometers and closing.

"Fire," said Riordan. "Load four missiles for second salvo. Load three missiles for third salvo, and include missile 1848 as the number-four missile."

"Missiles away," said the gunnery officer. "Second salvo targeted and loading. Third salvo targeted except missile 1848."

"Fire second and third salvos as fast as possible," said Riordan. "Then let's see what we hit."

He watched the first salvo tracking across the screen. The *Seattle* and the *Rubinstein* launched countermissiles, and directed laser fire at the incoming salvo. The *Wyoming* was also directing laser fire at the missiles. One of them exploded, obscuring the track of the missiles and the *Seattle*. Then the *Rubinstein* was hit. When the radioactive cloud dissipated a moment later, the *Rubinstein* was a slowly expanding cluster of fragments around a much larger fragment tumbling very slowly away from the *Vancouver*. The *Seattle* appeared unhurt. A salvo of six missiles was launched from the *Wyoming*.

"Salvos two and three launched," said the gunnery officer. "What targets, please?"

"Salvos four and five to the *Seattle*," said Riordan. "Direct laser fire at the *Wyoming*'s missiles. Hold the countermissiles until the last possible millisecond." He watched as the *Seattle* launched four missiles of her own. And the *Wyoming* launched a second salvo of six. For the first time he could smell the acrid fumes of discharged laser batteries as the *Vancouver* tried to destroy the attacking missiles. The room shook as something hit the ship.

"Salvo four launched," said the gunnery officer.

"Salvo five is loading on emergency power." He watched the *Vancouver*'s missiles moving across the screen. The situation screen was filled with missiles and countermissiles and radioactive haze and fragments of the *Rubinstein*, but he picked out missile 1848. It was moving away from all the tumult, and since it threatened nothing in the area, no one wasted a shot on it.

"That's for Joe Bob," he said softly.

The last thing he saw was missile 1848, safely on its way to Mundito Rosinante.

CHAPTER 9

Hulvey reached up and touched one of Dolores Ferranes's hands massaging his back.

"We're through to Administrator Bowman," said Corporate Elna, "you may want to use the telecon screen." Hulvey sighed, and walked over to the display desk behind the cameras and lights and telecon screens.

Administrator Stanley Bowman appeared, looking flushed and rather tense, and with him was Bob Schlecter. Schlecter was at the edge of the screening area, and the camera picked him up in profile. Hulvey shrugged. If Bowman wanted it in front of an audience, that's how he would get it.

"We have a mutiny in the fleet," Hulvey said without preamble, "the first reports are just coming in. It looks bad."

"What happened?" asked Schlecter.

"The senior officers in the L-5 Fleet are caucussing,

and the political officers—the ones we can reach—are talking about 'limiting the damage,' " said Hulvey.

"God damn them!" shouted Bowman. "They have the responsibility to prevent this shit! They have the authority to stop it! Tell them to start making arrests."

Hulvey glanced at the situation board his staff was working on, and winced. "That didn't work in the L-4 Fleet," he said. "We lost a lot of people trying. We took control of the NAUSS *Phoenix* and the NAUSS *Vancouver*, but we've lost contact with both ships."

"What do you mean, 'lost contact'?" asked Bowman.

"We're out of audio contact with both ships," said Hulvey wearily, "and the *Phoenix* don't show on the radar screens of any stations still responsive to our command." Off camera, Dolores fed hard copy to his desk, which sucked it in and pushed it out at him, as if it were a real desk. He took it. "Laputa radar reports that the *Vancouver* faded off the screen at 1534— about a minute ago." His eyes were suddenly blurred with tears, and he covered them with his hand as he fought to regain self-control.

"My son Dave, was the political officer on the *Vancouver*," Hulvey whispered. Dolores Ferranes fed his display desk another hard copy. He wiped his eyes and took it with wet and shaking fingers.

"The 4th Marine Division is preparing to embark on shuttles for Laputa. They will be ready to take off by 2400 hours at the latest, and they need flight clearance before then"—he reread the line in disbelief— "from NAUGA-Environment!" For some reason this struck him as hilariously funny, and he began to laugh. "Excuse me. The ozone layer is hardly a laughing matter, is it? It's just that we haven't had any sunspots late— lately—so we can't send up the Ma—Ma—" he dissolved in gales of laughter.

The President entered.

"I'll talk to Bannerman right away," said Schlecter. "That waiver has got to be expedited!"

"Don't bother, Bob," said the President, "I'm going to declare martial law."

Schlecter and Bowman stood up.

So did Hulvey, still laughing uncontrollably.

He stood there watching as the President declared martial law and ordered Bowman shot. After a while there was a sound offstage rather like a light bulb breaking.

"So much for Mortimer," said the President. "Now then, Hulvey, how did this trouble in the fleet start?"

Hulvey could never remember the rest of the interview. He answered questions mechanically, and in the end, it was just assumed that he was the Acting Administrator.

Acting Administrator William Hulvey sat in teleconference with Bob Schlecter of the Executive Office and Acting Fleet Admiral Nguen Tran Vong. Vong, wearing an undress khaki shirt with the wreath of five stars on the collar, had been forced on the Administration by the Loyalist officers of the L-5 Fleet.

"If you wish the fleet to survive," he said, in his flat Midwestern accent, "it will be necessary to eliminate a great deal of frivolity, particularly in the Political section."

"I wouldn't call the maintenance of political loyalty frivolous," said Hulvey.

"Not in theory," agreed Vong, "but in practice it has been destructive of morale and detrimental to operational efficiency."

"It worked well enough in the L-5 Fleet," said Schlecter. "Every major unit remained loyal to the NAU."

"Every major unit was also nonoperational, waiting funding for major maintenance or repairs," said Vong. "The L-4 Fleet, with honorable exceptions, went over to the mutineers. The political sections of both fleets were the same, and the results in each case were disastrous." He cleared his throat. "In one case a mutiny, in the other, inefficiency bordering on the pathological. I suspect that the L-5 Fleet would have mutinied had they not been tied to the umbilical supply line from Laputa."

"That borders on treason," growled Schlecter.

"So does the fleet," said Hulvey. "Get off his back, Bob."

"Thank you, Mr. Hulvey," said Vong. "Mr. Schlecter previously expressed the belief that the best way to insure the loyalty of the fleet was to keep it nonfunctional."

"I didn't say that!" protested Schlecter.

"Not in so many words," agreed Vong, "but I am not distorting your meaning. A nonfunctioning fleet, such as the NAU currently has, is a luxury we cannot afford. You must find better ways of insuring loyalty. You might, for example, reward excellence, diligence, and integrity above ideological purity."

"We must rebuild the fleet," said Hulvey. "How you do it is your business."

"Like hell it is," said Schlecter. He wiped his bald head with a handkerchief. "You can't ignore the political implications of what he wants to do."

"I don't like the humanists any more than you do, Bob," said Hulvey, "but I don't want to face a firing squad, either. Try to remember what *is* essential and what isn't, goddamnit! The fleet is essential!"

"Thank you again, Mr. Hulvey," said Vong. "We shall dispense with ideology. I also feel that the loyalty of the fleet is in question because the Government has questioned it at such length."

"It is necessary to test for loyalty," said Hulvey.

"One should not test to the point of destruction," replied Vong. "You also might seek to inspire loyalty instead of dread. Sullen obedience is useless in space."

"What would you suggest?" asked Hulvey.

"Alas, I have no suggestions," said Vong. He coughed again, a dry hacking sound. "I know the Navy, but not Security. At least couldn't you act like a legitimate government instead of a pack of thieves?"

"I doubt if the President will be pleased to hear that," said Schlecter.

"The men who told the President what he wanted to hear have served neither his interests nor theirs," said Vong politely. "In the L-4 Fleet they are dead."

"And in the L-5 Fleet we have accepted their resignations," added Hulvey. "Is there anything else?"

Vong checked his watch. "I must leave you very shortly," he said. "We all have much urgent business to attend to, but there is the matter of the bases."

"What bases, Admiral?"

"The ones that wish to remain loyal to the NAU, Mr. Schlecter," replied Vong, "except that they are enmeshed in ongoing Security investigations. I would have thought that to rally about in time of war was proof of loyalty." Vong smiled slightly. "I am, of course, not versed in Security procedures, but it would seem a pity to lose any more bases than we have to." Then he reached for the control, and just before turning himself off, gave them a formal quarter-bow.

"Do *you* know what he was talking about?" asked Schlecter.

Hulvey nodded. "A couple of our investigations were overtaken by events, is all."

"Well, then, Willy, you had damn well better play catch up, hadn't you?" said Schlecter, turning himself off. Hulvey stared at the blank screen for a moment, and shook his head.

"The Mayor of Los Angeles is on the line to see you," said Corporate Elna.

"About the plebiscite favoring union with Mexico?"

"Yes, sir. There were armed men in his office, so he may not be a free agent."

Hulvey sighed. "Right. What was it that Cantrell wanted for Mundito Rosinante?"

"If we would dismiss the charges against him with prejudice and convey title to the NAU half of the Mundito Don Quixote, he would declare for the NAU," said Corporate Elna. "He said it with legalistic precision in two and a half pages, but that's essentially it."

"Right," said Hulvey. "Dropping the charges is no

problem, but fill me in on Mundito Don Quixote. Where is it, and what does Cantrell want it for?"

Corporate Elna flashed a diagram on the screen, two concentric circles, the outer one blue, the inner one green. A red line was drawn from the center forming the radius of the blue circle, and then extended itself to form the diameter of the green circle. A blue dot appeared where the red line intersected the blue circle, with the label "Asteroid Rosinante," and at the other end of the line, on the green circle, a green dot appeared, labeled "Asteroid Don Quixote." The red line slowly rotated, turning on the center of mass, and after it had moved 60 degrees, a green triangle appeared on the green circle and began to chase after the green dot without ever catching it. The green triangle was labeled "Mundito Don Quixote." The red line made one full turn, and then a blue triangle, labeled "Mundito Rosinante" appeared on the blue circle, near the blue dot. It moved back and forth on chord drawn at right angles to the red line, a circular orbit viewed on edge.

"Mundito Don Quixote was destroyed by torquing in a union dispute," said the computer. "Cantrell probably wants to salvage what he can, and would like a clear title on whatever he finds."

"He'd run the salvage operation anyway," said Hulvey, rubbing his eyes. "Who has title now?"

"Title reverted to NAUGA-Treasury," said Corporate Elna.

"Give Cantrell what he wants," Hulvey said wearily. "And see that Vong gets an information copy. Do I have time to talk to Mayor Jackson?"

"Yes. The Senate hearing is running late."

Hulvey nodded, and the computer put the mayor through. After the mayor had said his piece, Hulvey studied him for a moment, and the red-bereted gunmen standing about his office.

"Last year," Hulvey said softly, "Southern California received 106 cubic kilometers of fresh water from the rest of the country. Think about it. That is a *lot* of water." One of the gunmen looked startled; perhaps he knew about irrigation. "That is one-fourth the volume of the Mississippi River devoted to Southern California," continued Hulvey, "and if you want that water *next* year, I suggest that you take your plebiscite and stick it up your ass!" He smiled, and turned himself off.

CHAPTER 10

The morning after the celebration that followed Mundito Rosinante's declaration of loyalty to the North American Union, Governor Charles Chavez Cantrell sat in his office feeling more than a little hung over.

"Good morning," said Marian Yashon, "are you ready to meet with the new at-large member of the Council?"

"Christ, no!" said Cantrell. "Even my hair hurts! When is he coming in?"

"Half an hour, maybe," she said. "Would you like some tomato juice artfully blended with puréed onion and other revolting stuff?"

"No. But I suppose I ought to drink it anyway." His strategist took a can from the refrigerator and poured it into a cup, adding a dash of dark liquid from a dark bottle, and stirring. He took it and began to drink very slowly.

"So now that we have title to the NAU half of Don Quixote," said Marian, "what are you going to do with it?"

"I don't know," said Cantrell, shaking his head and looking as if he regretted it. "You were the one that asked for it. What do *you* think we ought to do with it?"

"I don't know, either. I only wanted to keep other people from getting it. Maybe we could salvage something?"

"Do you know someone who wants to buy a billion square meters of broken-up plate glass?" asked Cantrell. He put his hand over his eyes. "Or twenty billion meters of composite-fiber reinforcement wire, slightly tangled?" He took a sip of his juice.

"Maybe something will turn up in the inventory," she suggested.

"Sure, Tiger, mirrors, motors, lots of stuff . . . but anything we need we already have. Maybe when the market goes up . . ."

"The price was right," said Marian.

Cantrell started to nod in agreement and checked himself. "Not if we picked the wrong side in a civil war."

"Don't worry about what's already been done," she said. "In a civil war all sides are wrong." Corporate Skaskash appeared on the telecom screen, projecting the image of Sir Alec Guinness playing a slightly sinister butler.

"Excuse me, sir," said the urbane Guinness voice, "a young gentleman to see you." The image looked down its nose at a card on the silver salver it held. "The Honorable Mr. W. Guthrie Moore, Member-at-Large from the Council."

"Send him in, Skaskash," said Cantrell.

W. Guthrie Moore walked in. He had a somewhat scraggly beard, and wore jeans and a red T-shirt. On the Tee shirt, in black, was stenciled a left fist over the initials MWPR. He looked to be about twenty. Cantrell stood.

"How do you do, sir," he said. "Will you have a chair?"

"I'll stand, Governor," said the youth.

"I thought the Ginger Group would have kept the council seat," said Marian. "How did you get it?"

"The Ginger Group split," said Moore, "and the losers joined the Popular Front. Which ran the MWPR candidate—me."

"Pardon my ignorance," said Cantrell, "but I never heard of the MWPR."

"It is the Marxist Workers Party of Rosinante," said Moore, "of which I am the secretary."

"Marx?" said Cantrell. "This is going to be one of those days." He started to shake his head and winced.

"Karl Marx, the Great Economist," said Moore, "who taught us to throw off the Chains of Oppression!"

"Marx is to economists what Khalil Gibran is to philosophers," said Skaskash unexpectedly. "In the real world there is no Marxist program, but inside the human brain he tickles the mood centers."

"What do you know about Marx?" said Moore.

"Quite a lot, actually," said Skaskash. "What do you know about economics?"

"I know we're being oppressed," said Moore, "and we're getting set to Rise in Our Might and Take Power."

"Really?" said Cantrell. "And will the MWPR include the workers who built Rosinante, and are hoping to enjoy the fruits of their labor?"

"No," said Moore, "those Running Dogs of Capitalism sold their birthright for a little property, and Property Is Theft!"

"That means your popular front is entirely Alamo students," said Marian, "and only the ones who sat around through all your stupid meetings, at that. Not even your Korean wives."

"We may be few," said Moore, "but we have Political Consciousness, and with Marxist Truth we shall prevail!"

"Marxist truth!" sneered Skaskash. "Marx himself didn't believe it!" An older or more experienced debater would not have risen to the taunt, but Moore had been a sophomore at Texas A&M prior to being sent to Mundito Rosinante in the corvée of students taken prisoner at the Alamo riots.

"Show me!" he said.

"Very well," replied Skaskash. "Karl Marx held two values above all others—the revolution and scientific truth." Moore nodded. "Second, Marx, a man of undoubted genius, died without ever finishing his magnum opus, *Das Kapital*. Mr. Moore, a genius does not die without finishing his life's work—I could cite you examples *ad nauseam*—but Marx lingered for years without finishing *Das Kapital*."

"So what?" said Moore. "He got old and sick and couldn't write, but what he wrote was the truth."

"No," said Skaskash. "The reason that Marx never finished his work was that his two prime values, revolution and scientific truth, were in conflict. He had, as you doubtless recall, set up a progression of social orders, from chattel slavery, to feudalism, to capitalism, to what he called socialism—a kind of unspecified utopia. In fact, there was another step after capitalism available for his study, but he suppressed it, because it was incompatible with his notion of revolution. He called it the 'Oriental Mode of Production' and it was amply demonstrated in Chinese history." The computer paused.

"You're supposed to ask: what is the Oriental Mode of Production?" said Marian. "I think you missed your cue."

"What was the Oriental Mode of Production?" asked Cantrell.

"I thought you'd never ask," said Skaskash. "It is capitalism made subordinate to the state by means of innumerable petty regulations. You could describe it as enlightened bureaucratic despotism, or as the symbiosis of the individual and the collective. Had Marx elected to follow scientific truth instead of revolution, he would have predicted what happened in the United States after the Great Depression. He would have been a major prophet. In the event, of course, he chose revolution, and is well on his way to becoming a demigod, a kind of secular Kali." Skaskash smiled slightly with the Guinness face. "The people truly devoted to Marx tend to be very similar to those truly devoted to Kali—the Thuggees, for instance."

"I don't believe you," said Moore, but without force.

"Look at your own soul," said Skaskash. "Did you not embrace Marxism as a means to legitimize violence?"

"Leave my soul out of this!" said Moore. "I don't have a soul any more than you do, you smart-ass tin can!"

"I have come to believe that I have a soul," said the computer affably. "It might even be immortal, although I doubt it."

"Would you like a cup of coffee, Mr. Moore?" asked Marian.

"No," said the youth, "I don't break bread with exploiters."

"I didn't offer you bread," said Cantrell. "However, you quoted Proudhon, saying 'Property is theft,' a little while ago. Consider Mundito Rosinante as a piece of property, if you will, and tell me who is its rightful owner—from whom was it taken?" He blew on his steaming coffee and took a tiny sip. "Do you and your Alamo students have a better claim than the working men and women who built it and were denied honest payment?"

"I am damn well not going to stand around bandying words with a bunch of fascist exploiters!" said Moore.

"You have presented your credentials," said Cantrell. "Good morning, sir."

"What's the next item on the agenda?" Cantrell asked, after Moore had gone.

"We just received a message from the L-4 Fleet," said Skaskash. "They took a tally of the missiles shot off during the mutiny, and they came up one short." Cantrell sipped his coffee and said nothing. "It was launched from the NAUSS *Vancouver*, bearing a one-megaton warhead. It is headed this way, and will arrive in about twenty-four days, according to the report."

Cantrell wiped the hot coffee off his fingers and desk with a tissue.

"That wasn't funny, Skaskash," he said. "Now stop clowning around!"

"Do you want hard copy?" asked the computer. "The message came in while you were talking to young Hotspur."

"No," Cantrell sighed. He took a sip of coffee. "Talk to NAUGA-Navy and find out all you can about the missile. Keep your line open to the L-4 Fleet, too. Maybe we can get the damn thing recalled."

"I wouldn't count on it," said Marian.

"I don't," said Cantrell, "but it doesn't hurt to try. You think it's from Joe Bob Baroody's group?"

"Yes. And probably aimed at the Prenatal Care Clinic."

"That would simplify the civil-defense problem," Cantrell said. "We'd know where to move the people away from. Skaskash, couldn't we turn our mirrors on the thing and melt it down before it gets here?"

"We can try. It will depend on the missile's cross section and velocity, and how fast and accurately we can work the mirrors." It paused for a moment. "I'll know when we get the specifics on the missile, but at the moment I kind of doubt it."

"Well, find out," said Cantrell. "We can figure out ways to minimize the damage, that's a straight engineering problem. But Marian, how are we going to break it to the people?"

To: NAUGA-Navy; ATTN: Adm. Nguen Tran Vong
Subject: Proposed Class II Base on Mundito Rosinante
From: The Executive Office
Date: 2 May 41

Enclosed is a digitized video recording from Gov. Charles C. Cantrell of Mundito Rosinante, playing time 195 seconds.

Cantrell asserts that GNM 1848 was launched from the NAUSS *Vancouver* during the L-4 Mutiny and is presently targeted on Mundito Rosinante. He asks that the GNM be diverted or deactivated.

Since we were recently at pains to insure that Mundito Rosinante declared its loyalty to the NAU, thereby insuring the feasibility of the subject item, this office feels that Gov. Cantrell's request is not unreasonable.

/s/

Randolph L. Hays, III
for Robert Schlecter
(enclosure)

To: Commander, L-5 Fleet; ATTN: V. Adm Foscari (acting)
Subject: GNM 1848
From: NAUGA-Navy, Office of C in C
Date: 3 May 41

(1) The attached memorandum is self-explanatory.

(2) Verify if GNM 1848 is indeed targeted on Mundito Rosinante.

(3) If this is the case, abort GNM 1848's mission immediately by any available means.

(4) Report on (2) and (3) immediately as information becomes available. Cite "Rosinante GNM."

/s/

Capt. H.Y. Lee
for Adm. Nguen Tran Vong

To: NAUGA-Navy; ATTN: Adm. Nguen Tran Vong
Subject: Rosinante GNM
From: L-5 Fleet, NAUSS *Duke Ellington*
Date: 7 May 41

Admiral Foscari has requested that we reply directly to your office on the subject item.

(1) GNM 1848 is targeted on Mundito Rosinante.

(2) GNM 1848 is responsive to the normal communications mode and is forthcoming on information

relating to location, course, configuration, and warhead. However, the computer has been reprogrammed to accept any further instruction in code only.

(3) The computer in GNM 1848 identifies this code as NIWRAD ARTNOC.

(4) This code is not listed in the Fleet Index of Codes, dated May '39. It is probably not a Fleet code at all, since Fleet codes routinely are indexed with a sixteen-digit entry.

(5) Since GNM 1848 is well beyond the range of laser fire or countermissiles, no action has been taken to implement (3) in your memo.

/s/
Lt. Cmdr. Burleigh Hill
Captain, NAUSS *Duke Ellington*

To: NAUGA-Security; ATTN: William M. Hulvey
Subject: Mundito Rosinante
From: NAUGA-Navy
Date: 11 May 41

The enclosed correspondence has a Priority-1 call upon your attention.

(1) GNM 1848 was launched from the NAUSS *Vancouver* at the time of the L-4 Mutiny, and is targeted on Mundito Rosinante.

(2) GNM 1848 was reprogrammed to accept further instruction in a non-Navy code only. This constitutes a major breach of security, unless of course the code originated in Security.

(3) If NAUGA-Security has access to this code, it is requested that NAUGA-Navy be permitted to use it to recall GNM 1848. If the code is regarded as highly sensitive, NAUGA-Navy will furnish the recall order for encryption and secure transmission.

(4) If NAUGA-Security does not have access to the code, we will have to consider the apportionment of responsibility for what is, I repeat, a major breach of security, the diversion from its lawful target of a Guided Nuclear Missile fired in anger.

With all due respect, a timely response would be appreciated. Cite "Rosinante GNM."

/s/

Capt. H.Y. Lee
for Adm. Nguen Tran Vong

Dolores Ferranes put out her cigarette as Administrator Hulvey entered his office.

"I've been waiting for you," she said. "Read these." She handed him the little sheaf of hard copy on GNM 1848.

"I'll get to them in a minute," he said. "First I need a drink."

"There's Coke in the fridge and rum in the liquor cabinet," said Ferranes. "How about a Cuba Libre?"

"You have one perverted sense of humor, Dolores," growled Hulvey. He put ice cubes in a glass and poured bourbon over them. "The President is dead set against giving up anything. The whole of Mexico is up in arms against us, and he's pretending to be Abraham Lincoln. How the hell did we ever get Mexico in the first place?" He stirred his drink with his finger and took a sip.

"In school they told us the Old Regime didn't build fission plants, so they needed Mexican oil," she said.

"God damn it!" said Hulvey. "How could they have been so frigging stupid as to take the Mexicans along with the oil?"

"That's ancient history, Mr. Hulvey," she said.

"Right." He took a swallow of bourbon. "Dolores, the thing about ancient history is that you need current events to understand what went on. Otherwise it's just incomprehensible. That stupid son of a bitch!"

"What bit of ancient history just now became clear for you?"

"Stalingrad," said Hulvey.

"Are you still trying to make policy?" Ferranes asked.

Hulvey finished his drink and reached for the bottle.

"That's enough!" snapped Ferranes.

"That isn't even close," sighed Hulvey, "but it'll do. What do you want?"

"Read the hard copy I gave you," she said, "and stop trying to hide in the bottle like poor old Stan."

Hulvey read through the little stack of memoranda. "Did you play Cantrell's speech?" he asked.

"He looks competent and didn't sound panicked," she said. "I strongly urge that we recall GNM 1848."

"Really?" He inspected the ice cubes in his glass and set it down on the Louis Quinze sideboard. "Explain, please."

"Basically, it's a chance to lay the Contra Darwin on the late Stanley Bowman," Ferranes said. "We recall the missile, and that is the end of it. Later, if anyone thinks to ask, we say we went through his papers and found the NIWRAD ARTNOC encryption key, and that will be the end of it. Too much is going on for anyone to go digging at a dead issue, and that will be the end of it, Mr. Hulvey!"

"You really want out of the Contra Darwin, don't you, Dolores?"

"Yes. Yes, my God, *yes*!"

"I kind of thought so. You don't think it's riskier to recall the missile than to just sit tight and say nothing?"

"Recalling the missile is a leap to safety. You take a chance, you win the reward. Sitting tight, you give your tacit approval to that missile. It is targeted on one of *our* Navy bases, and you can bet that it won't be forgotten if it isn't recalled!"

"Hell, Dolores, it won't be forgotten anyway."

"Unless it's recalled. Recalled, it would be just too embarrassing to think about, so we and the Navy will hide it under the rug. Otherwise, there *will* be an inquiry!"

"So what?" said Hulvey. "They won't find anything."

"Don't be an asshole!" screamed Ferranes. "The first thing they'll do is look to see who was in command of the *Vancouver* when the missile was shot off. It was your son, Riordan, your very own little boy! Next, they'll check out who could have reprogrammed the damned thing. Riordan, *again*! He was the P.O., and he'd just graduated from missile school! *Then* they'll look to see where the missile was aimed! They already *know*, Mr. Hulvey, but it hasn't registered yet! That missile is aimed at the Prenatal Care Clinic that Joe Bob died trying to blow up! Anytime anybody *looks*, it comes straight back to NAUGA-Security! Either Bowman or you! Recall the missile; you can lay the blame on Stan. Maybe they'll think you were in on it, but they can't prove anything, and nobody will want to take the lid off. You let that missile go, it *still* traces back to NAUGA-Security, only this time it isn't Bowman running the shop, Mr. Hulvey, *you* are running it! And this time the lid is *off*! A missile with a one-megaton warhead was put to private use! They can't ignore it! They *can't*!"

"They can't prove anything either way," said Hulvey quietly. "We can still blame Bowman if they come after us. We just couldn't find the encryption key, is all."

"*Jesus X. Christ*, Hulvey! You want the President to cut the country's losses, and you won't cut your *own*! Do you think anybody is going to worry about *proof*? In the middle of a civil war, someone uses a nuclear weapon and you say they can't *prove* it was you? Use your fucking head, Hulvey!"

"I'm going to have another drink. Can I fix one for you? We can toast the Contra Darwin."

"The Contra Darwin is *dead*, Hulvey!" Ferranes cried. "Joe Bob, Greene, Riordan, Stan—all *dead*! You want to drink their health?" She paused and took a deep breath. "Look. With three weeks' notice, do you suppose that whatever it is you're shooting at is going to stay put?"

"I don't care," said Hulvey. "Riordan died getting that missile off. He kept faith with me, I'm keeping faith with him."

"You are going to kill ten thousand innocent bystanders to keep the faith?"

"Yes," said Hulvey.

"Excuse me," said Dolores Ferranes. She walked swiftly to the bathroom.

Hulvey put fresh ice in his glass and poured himself another drink. Half an hour later his belt phone rang. He snapped it open.

"An ambulance is on the way to pick up Dolores," said Corporate Elna. "She has severe abdominal pains, diarrhea, and bloody stools."

"What's the matter with her?" asked Hulvey.

"My preliminary diagnosis is ulcerative colitis," said the computer. "As you may know, colitis is the psychosomatic illness that hits people who don't get psychosomatic illnesses."

"Well, look, is it serious?"

"Oh, certainly. The good news is that when Dolores was born, her placenta was frozen in liquid nitrogen and retained. In six months we can grow a new colon for her. The bad news is that she may not live six months."

"Merciful God," whispered Hulvey. "It hit her just like that?"

"The onset was sudden," agreed Corporate Elna, "but it was building for a long time. The ambulance has arrived. Will you tell the guards to admit the stretcher-bearers?"

CHAPTER 11

On May 3, 2041, Governor Cantrell convened the seven-member Council of Rosinante in his office for an emergency meeting.

Three members—Cantrell himself, Marion Yashon, and Corporate Skaskash—were appointed by the Charles C. Cantrell Foundation, which held 51 percent of the stock of Rosinante, Inc.

Two members—Ivan "Big John" Bogdanovitch and Don Dornbrock—were elected by Local 345 of the Space Construction Workers Union, which held title to four out of six purlins, and two out of four caps on Mundito Rosinante in lieu of unpaid back wages.

The minority stockholders of Rosinante, Inc., were represented by Corporate Forziati, a sophisticated computer, which, like Corporate Skaskash, manifested itself as an image on the telecon screen.

The Texas students of the Alamo corvée and their Japanese-Korean wives were represented by W. Guthrie Moore. He wore a black T-shirt proclaiming ALL POWER TO THE PEOPLE in yellow letters.

Cantrell walked into his office at precisely 0900 hours.

"Good morning," he said. "Coffee is available if you want it, and we have a selection of Danish on the serving cart. Please help yourselves." He sat down at the head of the conference table. "This meeting is going to be taped and will be rebroadcast locally. Any questions before we begin?"

"Yes," said Moore. "Why aren't we in the Council room?"

"Because we're still fixing the air-conditioning system in there," said Cantrell. "More questions?" He shrugged and folded his hands.

"Two days ago, on May 1," Cantrell continued, "I learned from Captain Lowell of the NAUSS *Ciudad Juárez* that we had a problem. Specifically, a missile had been launched from the NAUSS *Vancouver* during the L-4 Mutiny, and this missile, GNM 1848, was targeted on Mundito Rosinante with an E.T.A. of May 25, 2041. Naturally I had a few questions. We have enough answers to warrant this meeting. Corporate Skaskash will make a presentation of what we have, and we will, to the best of our ability, try to answer any questions *you* might have."

Corporate Skaskash, projecting the image of Humphrey Bogart, faded off the telecon screen at the foot of the conference table, and was replaced by a schematic diagram of the Solar System, red orbits on velvety black. A yellow dotted line traced an unnatural curve from the L-4 point of launch to the destination at Mundito Rosinante.

"This is the path that GNM 1848 is taking," said the Bogart voice. "It is moving under continuous low acceleration, which will cut off on May 21, right here." A yellow arrow appeared. "GNM 1848 will make its final approach coasting. We have no weapon that can reach it until it comes within range of our mirrors, at about 1,500 kilometers. At that time it will be closing with a velocity of $1,125 \pm 10$ meters per second, about 4,000 kilometers per hour, as it chases Mundito Rosinante in orbit."

"How do you know that this is the way the missile will approach?" asked Bogdanovitch.

"This is how GNM 1848's computer says it will approach," said Skaskash. "It is without guile, but unfortunately quite incorruptible. This approach is also calculated to minimize the effect of our mirrors." A diagram of Mundito Rosinante appeared on the screen, first full face, then rotating to the side view, showing the minimum aspect of its cross section. "We will have an effective heating time of approximately thirteen minutes, bringing the surface temperature of the missile to about 950°C, which will neither affect its maneuverability nor disable its bomb."

"I beg your pardon," said Corporate Forziati, "but I calculate that we will bring the missile's surface temperature to above 1400°C."

Both telecon screens flashed pages of calculations at each other.

"You appear to have calculated reflectivity on the basis of the mylar-aluminum mirror," said Skaskash after a moment. "In fact, we have a layered mirror that reflects red, blue, and green light to produce a synthetic white light that is very much cooler. Do you agree?"

"Yes," said Corporate Forziati. "Please continue."

"This is a diagram of GNM 1848 furnished us by NAUGA-Navy," said Skaskash, replacing the calculations. "If it has any weakness, it isn't immediately obvious. We will discuss active and passive countermeasures in a moment, but first let us consider the effect of the missile impacting as targeted."

The telecon screen now showed the side view and end view of the target cylinder.

"This is the outer end of the left-hand cylinder," said the Bogart voice. "It contains purlins four, five, and six. The missile is aimed at the window bay opposite purlin five, and will impact on it near the center of the window bay about five to twenty-five meters from the outer cap." A red X appeared on the diagram. "The missile penetrates the glass and moves toward purlin five at an angle of 6 degrees from the cap face." A dotted line appeared.

"According to NAUGA-Navy, the firing mechanism is operating in Mode 3. This means that the firing sequence is initiated by the shock of hitting the window glass, and, again according to the Navy, the firing sequence includes a five-second delay, which is intended to explode the one-megaton warhead right *here*, just above the Kyoto-Alamo in purlin five." The Bogart figure reappeared, smoking a fat tobacco cigarette. "If we don't do something about it, it could be serious. I don't have to tell you *how* serious, sweetheart."

"That isn't funny," said Moore. "The Kyoto-Alamo is where we live!"

"Right," said Skaskash. An animated sequence showed the explosion and its effects on the cylinder. "And *that's* the best case. Shall I continue?"

"No," said Moore. "What can we do about it?"

"We can begin by reducing the pressure to about 10mm by venting some 2,500 tons of oxygen in the envelope. This is done concurrently with reducing the spin, to bring the centrifugal force down to about 36cm/sec/sec."

"Are you also reducing the pressure in the purlins from one atmosphere to half an atmosphere?" asked Dornbrock.

"No," said Skaskash, "the purlins were built to withstand the envelope depressurizing, and leaving them fully pressurized makes the whole cylinder mechanically stronger. The second measure of passive defense is to change the aspect that the cylinder presents to the missile at the moment of impact. If the missile were to hit a purlin bay rather than a window bay, the firing sequence would be initiated as before, but the missile, after passing one hundred meters, would hit the purlin plate."

"You mean 'impact the purlin plate,' don't you?" asked Moore.

"The Inglese, she is the very difficult language to speak," said Skaskash. "However, we believe that when the missile hits the purlin plate it will detonate, blowing a hole about a kilometer in diameter in the purlin bay, and a hole 40 to 120 meters in diameter in the purlin plate and the soil it supports. Emergency repairs should prevent any substantial loss of pressure. We think that if the warhead attempts to follow the firing sequence the mechanism will deform to the point where it is inoperable."

"What if it does explode?" asked Moore.

"Then it would be exploding inside the already overpressurized purlin," said the Bogart voice, "with lamentable consequences. However, that case is not highly probable. Which brings us to active defense. Our mirrors, unfortunately, are inadequate. It is still possible, however, to interpose a shield between the missile and ourselves. Not a massive shield to deflect a nuclear explosion, but merely a few centimeters of glass to trigger the warhead prematurely. If we could explode it fifty or a hundred kilometers outside of the envelope, it would be harmless."

"Tell us about the shield," said Dornbrock. "I'd just as soon not have that mother exploding anywhere close."

"The material is salvaged from the wreckage of Mundito Don Quixote," replied the Bogart voice, "and what we are making is basically a sandwich, the bread being a pair of frames, twenty-two kilometers on a side. These frames are strung with the composite-fiber support wires, one every five centimeters. The meat of the sandwich is the broken envelope glass." The Bogart figure grinned, suddenly. "I have the plans and the work schedules. We can do it with time to spare if the Union will work three shifts on remotes!"

Bogdanovitch looked first at Skaskash and then at Cantrell.

"You're the Governor, Charlie. Why don't you just say: 'This has to be done!' and tell us to do it?"

"Because I can't pay you," said Cantrell. "I solicit your volunteer labor, but I cannot command it."

"But you're *Governor*," protested Dornbrock, "and this is like time of war!"

"Right," Cantrell agreed. "Only Rosinante isn't a republic or a country or a nation, but part of the NAU."

"Look," said Dornbrock, "if we go by the book, it will take the Union a week to vote on putting up that shield. We don't have the time. Can't you proclaim an emergency and *order* the Union to get to work?"

"I can," said Cantrell, "but I have no means to enforce that order. If I proclaim a state of emergency, will the Union go along with me?"

"Yes," said Bogdanovitch. "If you give the order, I will see that the Union raises the shield of Don Quixote."

"Can I ask a question, Governor?" said Moore.

"You just did," said Cantrell. "Want to ask another?"

Moore grimaced. "When is this emergency going to be over?"

"When the missile is disposed of, one way or another," replied Cantrell.

"That's going to be May 25," said Moore. "But look, first it was that guy, Joe Bob Baroody, and now it's GNM 1848 . . . both trying to hit the same end of purlin five, the end where *we* live. Who's doing it and why?"

"That's a good question, Mr. Moore," said Cantrell, "and I apologize for thinking you a fool. The answer is: I don't know. I don't know who, and I don't know why. I'll look into it, though, and report back to you in thirty days. Okay?

"In the meantime, a state of emergency is declared, to raise the shield of Don Quixote!"

After the Council of Rosinante departed, Cantrell sat in his office with Marian Yashon, folding and unfolding a little model of a purlin tile.

"What do you think, Tiger?" he said.

"Skaskash appears to have the missile crisis well in hand," she replied.

"Just as well," Cantrell said. "Do you think we'll get any action on the message I sent off to President Forbes?"

"Not before May 25," said Marian. "Moore asked the right question, you know. Who's shooting at us?"

"If we knew who, we'd know why," said Cantrell.

"You think we ought to question the Security people we took off the *Ciudad Juárez* some more?"

"They don't know anything," said Marian. "Even Terry didn't know anything. He wasn't part of the Baroody group, you know."

"Oh? That's why we killed the poor bastard."

"Right. But I reviewed all the actions on the ship involving Joe Bob, and one of them was his requisition for plastique—the plastic explosive stuff—and Terry turned it down."

"So?"

"So suppose Joe Bob *wasn't* trying to nuke the Prenatal Care Center. Suppose that little nuclear device we found in his bag was going to stay there, and he was using the explosive trigger as a demolition charge. Who was he after then? Or what?"

"Corporate Susan Brown," said Cantrell after a moment. He folded the model purlin tile shut with a snap.

"That's right," said Marian. "And plastique was his weapon of choice. Only Terry didn't approve the requisition for it. So Terry was after you, strictly according to orders, and Joe Bob was after Corporate Susan, strictly on his own."

"You know," said Cantrell after a moment, "when Gibson died—he's the one I named Joshua Willard for—in his last letter he said he'd had a run-in with Joe Bob Baroody posing as an MIS agent."

Marian walked over to the terminal and keyed in the file. After a minute, she looked up.

"So he did," she said. "What's more, Joe Bob turned up in connection with the IBM GR/W-42." She went back to the file. "The police report lists the cause of death as 'probable suicide.'"

"I never did believe that," said Cantrell, "but you know, when Corporate Susan arrived she had Gibson's signature on her invoice."

Marian turned again to the file.

"He signed the day after he died, didn't he?" she said. She got up and drew herself a cup of coffee, adding cream and sugar. "Suppose the Baroody group was after Corporate Susan—what then?"

"Then I suppose they still are," said Cantrell softly. "GNM 1848 is like Thoreau's trout in the milk."

"What?"

"Convincing circumstantial evidence. In Thoreau's time, watering milk was a common cheat."

"Water comes from faucets," said Marian, "and trout comes from the frozen-food counter. I don't make the connection."

"At that time a farmer would often get water from the stream."

"And trout swim in the stream. . . ." Marian paused. "You mean a live trout in your milk?!"

"Or a freshly dead one," said Cantrell. "The evidence that your milk had been watered."

"I see," Marian nodded. "Someone in the Baroody group was on the *Vancouver* to shoot off the missile." She sipped her coffee. "I'll get the T/O and see if any of the names look familiar. Maybe the Security people from the *Ciudad Juárez* can tell us something, after all."

"That's one place to look," he agreed. "And wasn't Senator Gomez tying Joe Bob to whatshisface, the fellow heading up NAUGA-Security—Bowman?"

"That may have been why the Senator's plane crashed," said Marian.

"Say it was true," said Cantrell. "That means the Baroody group went right to the top of NAUGA-Security."

"Maybe," said Marian, sipping her coffee. "Of course, the charges that they put in against you were trash. That had to come from the top, I would think." She put her coffee down and sat back in her chair. "I believe Hulvey, the Deputy Administrator, is acting as Administrator right now."

"Oh? What happened to Bowman?"

"I've heard rumors that he's dead," she said. "Nothing official, of course. But I haven't asked, either." She pulled at her lower lip. "Yet. I wonder why Corporate

Susan Brown has all these violence-prone people after her?"

"You don't suppose she—it, I mean—would have any idea, do you?" said Cantrell.

"It couldn't hurt to have a little talk with her," agreed Marian.

CHAPTER 12

"I'm sorry," said Corporate Elna, in precise obedience to orders, "but the Administrator is in conference with the President and cannot be disturbed. Can I leave a message?"

"No, thank you," said the caller, a paratroop captain in field uniform, "I'll try again this afternoon."

In fact, Administrator Hulvey had simply walked away from his official duties for a little while, and was across town visiting Dolores Ferranes at the University of St. Louis Hospital.

Dolores had a private room, done in beige and dark beige, the woodwork pointed up with white enamel. It was a quiet room, a tranquil room with two windows overlooking a courtyard that had flowering white dogwoods in concrete pots set around a little pool with lily pads and goldfish.

When Hulvey came in, she was sitting in the easy chair reading Shakespeare's *Julius Caesar*.

"Hello, Willy," she said cheerfully. "Nice of you to pop over."

"I was at the tobacconist's shop," he said, "but they

only had pipe tobacco and cigars, so I brought you a plant, instead." He took an African violet out of its paper bag and set it on the windowsill. "All you have to do is keep the reservoir filled and check the idiot lights; the pot takes care of everything."

"Just the thing for a busy executive," she said, "but I'll have time to fuss with my plants now, Willy. Did Corporate Elna give you my application for disability retirement?"

"Yes," said Hulvey, "but I don't think you ought to let a nervous stomach throw you. I'd much rather give you all the advance sick leave you need and have you back in six months or a year."

"Willy, my darling," said Dolores gently, "I love you. But I'm not coming back."

"What do you mean, you aren't coming back? I need you!"

"What for, Willy? The best advice I can give you, you can't take." She took a little wooden machine out of the drawer and poured a measure of tobacco into it from a pouch. Then she turned the handle and it rolled a cigarette for her. She put the machine back in the drawer and lit the cigarette with a permanent match sitting on the table.

"My office chipped in and bought me these," said Dolores. "Did you know that I can't roll a cigarette anymore? Or strike a kitchen match on my thumbnail? My nervous stomach, as you call it, has chewed ulcers through the wall of the colon, and the wastes and poisons are leaking through the ulcers into the bloodstream. Where they have been hitting the joints in my hands and feet. I have arthritis now, but the doctors don't think the damage is permanent. Once my new colon is grown and implanted, it should clear up."

"Well, you can come back then," said Hulvey. "Or come back as a rehired annuitant, if you'd rather."

"No, Willy. I used to think that death wouldn't release me from the Contra Darwin. Maybe it won't, but my body can't run the course anymore. If I went back all healed up, my new colon would be shot inside three months." She flicked the ash into her cobra ashtray.

"You smoke too much," growled Hulvey.

"The doctor says as long as I don't inhale through the rectum it's all right," she said. "It wasn't tobacco that did me in, it was stress—and smoking was one way to ease it." She smiled and brushed her hair back. Hulvey noticed that there was quite a lot of gray showing. "My job is stressful. Most of the time NAUGA-Security is involved in the gray areas of the law. They have to get results, and I have to keep them clean. When you reactivated the Contra Darwin on top of that, it was just too much. If I went back, what would I find?"

"You can watch the news on the tube," said Hulvey. "I don't suppose you want to hear the latest on the other."

She blew a smoke ring. It rolled through the air, and disintegrated in a vagrant breeze from the air conditioning.

"No," said Dolores at last, "I don't want to know. I'm starting to hurt just talking about it."

Hulvey's belt phone rang. He snapped it open.

"The President has just been assassinated," said Corporate Elna. "Don't, repeat, DO NOT come back to the office. The place is full of paratroops."

"Oh really?" said Hulvey. "Suppose I meet you for lunch—where would you suggest?"

"Try the Arnstein Police Barracks," said Elna. "It's ten minutes' walk from the hospital. Get moving!" The connection clicked off.

"That will be fine," said Hulvey, "I'll see you then." He snapped the phone shut, and turned back to Dolores.

"I'll sign your disability retirement," he said, "but I've got to run."

She put out her cigarette and stood up with a visible effort.

"Good-bye, Willy. Take care of yourself."

At the door he started to shake her hand, and then leaned over and kissed her on the cheek.

"Good-bye, Dolores," he said, "you gave it all you had."

CHAPTER 13

Corporate Susan Brown manifested itself on the telecon screen as an attractive young woman with dark blond hair. She wore a white lab coat with a stethoscope around her neck, and a tiny bit of vivid green blouse showing.

"What can I do for you?" asked the computer in a well-modulated contralto.

"We have a problem," said Cantrell. He sat at his desk, flanked by the flags of Rosinante and the NAU. Skaskash had offered to set the mirrors to backlight the window behind his desk, but Cantrell declined. The psychology of computers was hard to estimate. He shrugged. "The problem is political rather than medical, and I don't know whether or not you can help."

"You've heard of GNM 1848?" asked Marian.

"Of course," said the contralto voice. "I seek to be aware of my environment as much as possible."

"Splendid," said Marian. "We believe that GNM 1848 and the incident with Joe Bob Baroody are related. We also believe that you are the target in both cases. Can you say why this might be so?"

"I am afraid not," said Corporate Susan. "I am aware, of course, that Joe Bob destroyed a previous incarnation of my machinery, and that in so doing he killed the woman whose face and voice I now use. I surmise that he was a religious fanatic. I can imagine no cause for GNM 1848."

"Religious fanaticism covers a multitude of sins," said Marian. "I notice that you used the word 'incarnation' with respect to your machinery."

"The word seems apt," said the computer. "Would you have preferred that I describe myself as 'overhauled' or 'rebuilt'?"

"That's hard to say," Marian conceded. "Possibly I would have described Dr. Susan Brown as reincarnated and you extensively retrofitted and redesigned, but I'd hardly insist on the words."

"Nor do I," said the computer. "As you know, I have the capability to manipulate genetic material. I can read and write DNA, if you wish, and to some people this gives offense."

"To the point of using nuclear weapons?" asked Cantrell.

"I find it hard to believe that GNM 1848 could be in any way connected with the late Joe Bob Baroody," said the computer.

"The connection is conjectural," said Marian, "but Baroody was also Lieutenant Holt, who was a member of the Military Intelligence Service, which is an arm of NAUGA-Security, which in turn is headed up by Stanley Bowman, who, as it happens, was acquainted with Joe Bob back in the days of the Creationist Coalition."

"Bowman is dead," said Corporate Susan.

"I've heard that," said Cantrell, "but nobody will confirm it."

"His obituary appeared in the St. Louis *Star-Post* on May 4, 2041," said the computer. "It gave the date of birth, position at time of death, and listed the cause of death as 'sudden.' "

"It didn't list the date of death?" asked Cantrell. "Curious."

"It is curious," agreed Marian. "However, Bowman was replaced as the Administrator of NAUGA-Security by his Deputy Administrator, William M. Hulvey, and he in turn was the father of Commander Riordan Hulvey, the P.O. on the NAUSS *Vancouver*, and the officer in command when GNM 1848 was launched."

"Someone on the *Vancouver* was responsible," agreed the computer, "but perhaps not Commander Hulvey. Since they are all dead, it is impossible to check."

"I offered conjecture, not proof," said Marian. "And again, I ask you if you have any idea why you are drawing this fire?"

"Your conjecture is interesting," said Corporate Susan, "but I really have no idea. The idea that there is a conspiracy out to get me seems paranoid."

"Look," said Cantrell, "you're doing an outstanding job operating the local health services. I want to keep you around. But I'm also trying to find out why we're getting hit. Perhaps it would concentrate your thinking if we asked you to show cause why you should not be shipped back to Tellus."

"Perhaps," agreed the computer. "But since I have been fully cooperative with you," the figure on the screen flashed a truly dazzling smile, "I rather doubt it."

The Shield of Don Quixote was fashioned in this manner. The front of the shield was an array of tetrahedrons made from the spun beams salvaged from the main frame of Mundito Don Quixote. It measured 22 by 25 by 0.80 kilometers. On the outer face of the shield were mounted nine fixed rocket engines to maneuver the shield in place, while around the perimeter were eight smaller engines, mounted on universal joints, to orient the shield in space. On the inner face of the shield was laid a mat of composite-fiber reinforcing wire that was to support a layer of broken plate glass.

It is of interest to describe the wire and the process by which it was manufactured. The carbon mined from the Asteroid Rosinante, a carbonaceous chondrite, was processed *in situ* to nylon-413. The nylon-413 was then oriented and carbonized to graphite fiber. The graphite fiber was then exposed to silane, SiH_4, at low pressure and high temperature to deposit a thin film of silicon on the graphite fiber's surface. Heat treatment then reacted carbon and silicon to form silicon carbide, so that the fibers could now be wetted with an aluminum alloy, Al 95 percent, Si 4.8 percent, Ge 0.2 percent, which formed the matrix for the graphite–silicon carbide fibers. This wire, 1.25 millimeters in diameter, was wound on huge spools holding 220 kilometers of wire.

On top of the layer of glass was placed a keeper, a rectangular frame of beams 22 by 25 kilometers, which was strung with the composite-fiber reinforcing wire, spaced at 5-centimeter intervals along the 25-kilometer side. A curious construction detail: the keeper was fastened on the 25-kilometer side with a combination hinge and latch so that it could be opened from either "top" or "bottom." The purpose of the keeper was to keep the broken plate glass from sliding off the face of the shield when the shield was being maneuvered into position.

The men and women of the Union, working around the clock with remotes and in suits, completed the Shield of Don Quixote and brought it into position forty-nine hours and ten minutes before the projected impact time of GNM 1848. Governor Cantrell gave each of them the same Rosinante Defense Medal that had been given to the Rosinante Militia after the capture of the NAUSS *Ciudad Juárez*.

Curiously enough, the militia did not resent this, and the workers did not feel the gesture was insulting.

The residents of the Kyoto-Alamo were moved to the inner cap of the left-hand cylinder for safety. At first there was talk of "evacuating" them, but since the envelope of the left-hand cylinder was also being evacuated, it was decided that people "moved." Following his constituents, Governor Cantrell set up his emergency headquarters in the same place.

Actually, his emergency headquarters consisted of his Oriental carpet and the desk from his office plus a patchwork of communications equipment. Corporate Skaskash was in charge of the defense, and Cantrell, like everyone else, had to stand by and watch. As Governor, however, he had the privilege of asking questions of Skaskash, and he was part of the televised show. All of Rosinante would see what he saw as soon as he saw it, and they would also see how he reacted.

"Twenty-nine minutes and counting," said Skaskash. "We are very close to the point where GNM 1848 will be unable to maneuver around the shield."

"We have a burn," said a woman's voice.

"The missile initiated evasive action at minus 28:40," said Skaskash. "It is moving on the Y-axis in a positive direction."

"Burn terminated after 1.72 seconds," said the woman.

"Good morning, GNM 1848," said Skaskash politely. "Do you read me?"

The reply appeared as letters floating across the telecon screen.

"Affirmative," they read. "How may this missile be of service?"

"What is your fuel reserve, and how are you going to use it?" asked Skaskash.

"This missile has the equivalent of 33.15 seconds of burn," replied GNM 1848, "of which 31.00 will be expended in a burn initiated at minus 44.06 seconds."

"Thank you, sweetheart," said the Bogart voice. "This is the updated situation, Governor Cantrell," it continued. "Please observe the situation screen." The situation screen was velvety black with yellow axes marked X and Y. "The target appears as the small green circle at the origin." A circle appeared. "The shield is represented by this thin green line 50.0 kilometers distant. Note that the shield extends 11 kilometers above and below the X-axis. The red dart is GNM 1848. Formerly it was moving along the X-axis, and would have hit the shield and exploded at a safe distance. Now, however, it will follow the red dotted line to just above the shield, at which time it will initiate its 31-second burn to hit the target."

"How close will it come to the shield?" asked Cantrell.

"Between 100 and 200 meters," said Skaskash, "dead center on the even edge."

"Very interesting," replied Cantrell. "And what are you going to do about it?"

"Release the odd-numbered keeper catches," was the answer. "Did you ever find out why the Navy failed to recall or abort the missile?"

"No," said Cantrell. "Anyway, you'd be the first to know, wouldn't you?"

"Probably," agreed the Bogart voice. "I heard from the L-4 Fleet that the missile code had been changed so the Navy couldn't control it. A rumor, perhaps."

"Perhaps not," said Cantrell. "They never said anything, the Navy. They might have been embarrassed."

"Odd keeper latches released except 39 and 71," said a woman's voice.

"I have 71," said a man's voice.

"We going to pry 39 loose," said someone else. Then, "Okay, we have her open."

"Prepare to extend keeper," said Skaskash.

"What are you doing?" asked Cantrell, exactly as they had rehearsed it.

"Take a look, sweetheart," said Skaskash. The diagram on the situation screen changed. The origin was now surrounded by a large green circle with the purlins indicated as arcs shaded solid green. The shield was a heavy green line at the right side of the telecon screen. A red dotted line, marked PATH OF GNM 1848, eased over the top of the shield and bent down to hit the center of purlin bay six. A thin green line, the keeper hinged at the top of the shield, slowly separated itself from the bottom and moved like the hand of a clock toward nine. As it did so, it crossed the red dotted line.

"The keeper is strong enough to deflect the missile," said Skaskash. "I expect that the path of GNM 1848 will be modified something like this." The dotted red line was redrawn parallel to the thin green line of the keeper and passed above the green circle as it went off the left side of the telecon screen.

"What if it isn't?" asked Cantrell.

"We'll see," was the reply. "Extend the keeper at half-speed, please."

Cantrell snapped open his belt phone and pushed the button for Marian Yashon.

"How is it playing in the peanut gallery, Tiger?" he asked.

"Things are pretty calm," she said. "What people are talking about is the Ginger Group's recall initiative. They claim that Moore was improperly nominated, and Skaskash has agreed to rule on the question when he isn't so busy."

"Politics as usual, eh?" Cantrell said. "I can't say I'd be sorry to see Moore off the Council, though."

"They could find worse," said Marian.

At minus 15 minutes the mirrors began tracking GNM 1848, and the situation board began recording the temperature readings.

At minus 12 minutes, the keeper was fully extended. One or two pieces of plate glass drifted slowly away from the back face of the shield, flashing in the mirror-concentrated sunlight.

"Wasn't the angle between shield and keeper supposed to be 90 degrees?" asked Cantrell. "It looks bigger."

"It is," agreed Skaskash, "about 94 or 95 degrees. When we rotated the mass of the keeper, it pushed against the mass of the shield. The keeper moved a lot while the shield moved only a little. However, the keeper is where it is supposed to be."

At minus 54 seconds, the woman began a countdown.

"We have a burn," she announced, as GNM 1848 started its ignition sequence. Cantrell watched as the missile began to move through the keeper.

"Fire on the keeper!" shouted the woman.

"What the hell happened?" asked Cantrell. The solid red line, which was tracking the actual path of the missile, extended itself between the dotted line that GNM 1848 had sought to follow, and the dotted line that Skaskash had tried to impose upon it. A second solid red line appeared at the end of the keeper, diverging from the first at a small angle. Both vanished off the left side of the screen far above the green circle. Cantrell's belt phone rang.

"Listen to them cheer!" Marian was shouting to make herself heard above the joyous noise in the background.

"Hey, Skaskash!" shouted Cantrell, "You did it! What the hell happened at the end? What was the fire?"

"The missile was heated to 937° C, and moving at 1,142.4 meters per second when it touched the keeper wires," said Skaskash. "The impetus from the rocket pushed it into the wires, which acted like sawblades. The keeper wires sliced the missile like a boiled egg, and when the wires reached the fuel tanks at minus 25 seconds or so, the fuel and oxygen combined and blew up. The sliced up warhead went one way, and the rocket engines went the other. Shall we have a party to celebrate?"

"She-it!" shouted Cantrell. "We did it!"

"Charles!" came Marian's voice, very faint over the belt phone. "The cleanup, Charles!"

"What about the cleanup?" asked Cantrell.

"We have to repressurize the envelope and pump up the spin again," said Skaskash. "And the shield will have to be moved, of course."

"Wasn't it drifting away from the Mundito?" asked Cantrell.

"Yes, but we corrected that," replied Skaskash. "Retract the keeper at half-speed, please. After the keeper is retracted, latch and maintain orientation and position until we refuel."

Cantrell hit the telecon button for Union Headquarters. Bogdanovitch appeared on the screen, holding a bottle of champagne that was spurting over hand and glass.

"Hey, Big John!" shouted Cantrell. "I'll drink to that!" He looked around. His office refrigerator remained in his office. Here there was only a thermos of coffee. He didn't want coffee.

"What is it, Charlie?" asked Bogdanovitch, spraying champagne around.

"I wish I had some of that," Cantrell said drily. "Whenever you're ready, Big John. You can start to pump up the spin and repressurize the envelope whenever you're ready."

"Right away, Charlie!" Bogdanovitch shouted. He emptied the bottle over Dornbrock's head, grinning hugely.

CHAPTER 14

St. Louis, May 25, 2041. Burning armor stained the blue spring sky with black smoke. Most of the city was untouched, but around the Federal District the streets were littered with the debris of war. Concertina wire, broken glass, shell casings of various sizes, pockmarked building façades—all spoke of recent fighting. A paratrooper dusted with quicklime lay beside a recoilless rifle to give mute testimony of *how* recent.

An armored personnel carrier rolled up to the parking garage of the motel where Hulvey had his field headquarters, the guard waving it to enter. The driver opened his window.

"I *can't* go in," he said. "The clearance is only two meters."

The guard spoke into his phone. Presently William Hulvey came out, accompanied by a number of officers. They marched over to the back of the APC, the door opened, and a sergeant and a medical officer helped a small man, unshaven and in rumpled civilian clothes, step down.

"How do you do, Dr. Oysterman," said Hulvey. "If you will be so kind as to follow me, I'll see if we can't arrange a shave and a shower and perhaps a change of clothes for you."

"Ah . . . yes. That would be nice . . . I think," said Dr. Henry Oysterman, looking vaguely about him. "I can't see too well without my glasses, but . . . but don't I know you?"

"Certainly, sir. My name is William Marvin Hulvey, Administrator of Security. We've met often."

"Oh yes—yes, of course," said Oysterman. "I remember you very well. You and the President used to have the most awful arguments—about Mexico, I believe . . ." Hulvey waved off the sergeant, and with the medical officer led Oysterman gently into the motel.

"Yes, yes, of course—I remember very well, Mr. Hulvey. You wanted to let Mexico go its own way, and the President wanted to hold the Union together. You were right. I always admired you for . . . for speaking up, you know. Everybody else was afraid of President Forbes—I know I was." He fumbled in his pockets for a moment. "Dear me, I seem to have forgotten my glasses. Or lost them . . . I don't exactly remember."

"It doesn't matter," Hulvey told him. "We'll get you new glasses as soon as we can." He turned to the medical officer. "Is the Vice President all right?"

"He seemed a little disoriented when we rescued him," was the reply. "He might be in a mild state of shock. Aside from minor cuts and bruises, I don't see anything wrong with him, though."

"Good," said Hulvey. "I want him sworn in as President this afternoon. Here's his room. Get him cleaned up and made presentable." He turned to one of his officers. "Major Fisher. Find Dr. Oysterman's prescription and have a new set of glasses made up for him." His belt phone rang.

"I'm putting through Lieutenant Chen," said Corporate Elna.

"We've just taken Brigadier General Carney, sir!" said Lieutenant Chen. "What shall we do with him?"

"Shoot him. Corporate Elna will get some press to cover the event, but I want you to stand him up against a wall and shoot him. A south-facing wall, so the son of a bitch has the sun in his eyes. I'm much obliged to you, Captain Chen, I'm much obliged." He snapped the phone shut.

"That leaves the Black Muslim, Brigadier General Daoud," said Hulvey, "the last of the four generals."

"We'll have him by nightfall," someone said.

"We'll see," said Hulvey. "Now that we have a President, Colonel, suppose that you arrange a teleconference with Pablo Cuevas for me?"

"Sir? You want to talk to *Cuevas*, sir?" the colonel was scandalized.

"Not really, but I have to talk to someone in MUFF, and starting with Cuevas will maximize the annoyance on the other side." Hulvey shook his head. "Subjectively, it is the move most disagreeable to the opposition. I am sure they would much prefer three or four years of war coming to the same conclusion. Señor Cuevas might *insist* on his war, but if so he will get it from his fellow revolutionaries, not from me."

The wardroom aboard the SS (formerly NAUSS) *Ciudad Juárez* was paneled with redwood burl-pattern hardboard, and the redwood burl formica tables were covered with nonwoven damask pattern tablecloths. One end of the room had been partitioned off with a sliding fiberglass screen, behind which a teleconference booth had been improvised. At the other end of the room a teletypewriter was churning out hard copy on selected subjects, and these were posted on a large bulletin board which stood between the teletype and the wastebasket.

The ship's Executive Officer, Commander Martin Rogan, was reading directly from the printer when the screen slid back and Captain Robert Lowell stepped across the room into the head. After a moment the toilet flushed and Lowell reappeared to undo the work of a moment before by pouring himself a cup of coffee, which he took black with two envelopes of sugar. He was a young man, not yet thirty, but with a face one couldn't say that was any age at all.

"What's new, Captain?" asked the Executive Officer.

"The forces of anarchy and chaos are having trouble getting organized, Mr. Rogan," said Lowell. He seated himself at the table nearest the teleconference booth, and blew on his steaming coffee cup. "Right now we are taking a break. What's new in the real world?"

"Reuters confirms the report that Brigadier Mohammed Daoud is dead," said Rogan. "According to Reuters, he was attempting to escape aboard a shuttle, and when its takeoff was prevented, he shot himself in the men's room."

"I suppose that's the Army way," said Lowell with a perfectly straight face. "An Admiral would have shot himself in the head."

"Yes, Captain Lowell," said Rogan, wondering if he should laugh.

"Well, that's the end of the four generals," said Lowell, taking a tiny sip of his coffee. "A pity things didn't work out for them. We might have been mutually helpful."

"I thought we put them up to it," said the Executive Officer. "All the papers said so."

"Don't believe everything you see on hard copy," said Lowell. "Besides, how many generals do *you* know?"

"I don't know any," said Rogan.

"Nor do I," said Lowell, "although it's true we set them a bad example. Still, one would expect the Army to show better sense than to do as the Navy did. Was there anything about the new President?"

"Dr. Oysterman?" Commander Rogan looked through the hard copy. "Here. He offered to negotiate Mexican Independence."

"Oh really?" Lowell looked interested. "What sort of offer did he make?"

"Reuters again," said the Executive Officer. "He appointed Hulvey as his chief negotiator." He read a bit further. "Hulvey was maybe a crackerjack security man, but he doesn't know shit about negotiating. He told MUFF right up front that Mexico would be getting Texas, New Mexico, and Arizona, except for the northwestern corner. He expects to keep California."

"Pardon my ignorance, Mr. Rogan, what is MUFF?"

"The Mexican United Freedom Front," replied Rogan. "It's a coalition. They'll never let Hulvey hang on to California, and he'll never get back what he put on the table."

"Really, Mr. Rogan? And what did MUFF say to this offer?"

"WP this time," said the Executive Officer, "Pablo Cuevas of the Radical Intransigent Party said yes. Carlos Montez of the Reformed Mexican Marxist Workers Party said they must have California also. The central committee of the Pan Hispanic League said they want California and also Cuba and Florida. The Reborn Trotskyite Party"—he turned the page—"calls for Victory or Death. MUFF issued a joint communiqué, calling Hulvey the worm in a poisoned apple, but saying that they were not refusing to negotiate."

"What a pack of clowns," said Lowell, taking a sip of coffee. "Hulvey is going to take the lot, you watch."

"He can't," said Rogan, "Los Angeles has more Chicanos than Mexico City. No way can the NAU hang on to California."

"Sure there is, Mr. Rogan," said Lowell, sitting back. "Think about it. Hulvey has already said what the borders are going to be. And he still has control in the disputed area. I would expect that you are going to have Anglos going one way and Chicanos going the other—maybe under pressure. By the time MUFF gets its act together, the Texas Anglos are going to be in California, and the California Chicanos are going to be in Texas. And then MUFF can do whatever it damn well pleases, because the NAU is going to have Anglos on the borders that Hulvey has chosen."

"That's what—maybe thirty million people moving back and forth?" Rogan shook his head. "It will never happen."

"You think not?" said Lowell. "Do you know what the L-4 Fleet Caucus was discussing just now? Whether or not to permit free movement of L-4 Anglos to L-5, and L-5 Chicanos to L-4. Somehow, people want to segregate with their own kind, and the idea seems to have taken hold that the L-5, under the NAU, is going to be Anglo." He took a sip of coffee. "I have been in favor of free movement. The NAU is dead, no matter what they call the Government that President Oysterman is heading up. Why keep the old ratios and job quotas? Why keep job quotas at all, now?"

The air conditioning having been renovated, the Council Chamber was comfortable. The arching blue mirrors still echoed the clerestory windows on the other side of the room, but the slowly revolving fans that hung from the lofty white ceiling were purely decorative, elaborate supports for the nonfunctional Tiffany lamps. The massive Council table had been removed while the work was in progress, and since the doors had been narrowed by the inclusion of air ducts in the wall it could not be gotten back in. The Council of Rosinante sat around one of the folding tables from the Executive Dining Room.

Despite the room's coolness, however, W. Guthrie Moore was hot. He stood before the Council in black denim jeans and black Wellington boots with heel plates, a black leather jacket lavishly decorated with metal studs and a red T-shirt with a left fist raised over the slogan: VIVA LA REVOLUCIÓN! If clothes made the man, here was a fire-eating revolutionary, and he expressed his profound displeasure at being arbitrarily and unjustly removed from his Council seat.

"You lousy bastards robbed me blind!" he said. "There wasn't no need to call no special election! The one we had was fair enough!"

"The Ginger Group objected to the nominating procedure," said Cantrell, "and some of your tactics were, as Judge Skaskash said, unconscionable."

"We went strictly according to the book," said Moore. "You can read the minutes if you don't believe me."

"The minutes were contravened by sworn testimony," said Cantrell. "You could be held in contempt for failing to obey a court order that called for new nominations as well as new elections, you know."

"Since there was a write-in candidate, that question is moot," said Marian. "If you had half a wit, you'd give it up."

"Never you mind about my wits, you fat old bag!" snapped Moore. "The whole thing was a put-up job, trying to keep power from the People! *I* am the only People's Candidate! That tin-can baby doctor is a fucking fake!"

"Really, Mr. Moore?" The image of Corporate Susan Brown raised an eyebrow with exquisite precision. "My constituents are the women of Rosinante, whom I serve as gynecologist, obstetrician, and pediatrician. All the women, not merely your Oriental wives. Are you saying that women aren't people?"

"I'm saying I was robbed, you lying bitch!"

"You'd call a buzzsaw a bitch if you backed into one," said Corporate Susan. "Your choice of words suggests sadly inadequate programming."

"Shut up, you reactionary hunk of junk! When the people rise up in their might, *you* are going in the dustbin of history—or maybe the garbage disposal!"

"*What* people, Mr. Moore?" The menace in Corporate Susan Brown's voice was astonishing. "That shabby clique of role-playing radicals that calls itself the Popular Front? They still haven't admitted they aren't in Texas. Or your tiny coterie of sexually kinky friends? *They* think a political movement begins with the pelvis and ends at the anus!"

Moore flushed and hit Corporate Susan a back-handed swipe across the telecon screen, leaving a slight scuff on the plastic surface.

"Real Texas macho," said Corporate Susan. "A woman gives you lip, hit her a good one. A woman tells you something you don't want to hear, knock her mouth shut. Well, listen up good, you silly son of a bitch, I'm *not* a woman, and if you give me any more shit I'm going to deball you without anesthesia!"

"A little order, please," said Cantrell. "You're a sore loser, Guthrie, but you're still a loser. It's likely just as well you aren't on the Council anymore. If you are lucky, our paths won't cross again.

"I believe the question before the Council is: shall we seat Corporate Susan Brown as the duly elected at large member?"

"Move the question," said Corporate Forziati.

"Second the motion," said Corporate Skaskash.

"The goddamned machines have more solidarity than people!" said Moore.

"I believe it would be appropriate to take a record vote," said Cantrell.

"Yes," said Marian Yashon.

"Yes," said Corporate Skaskash.

"We discussed this in the Union," said Dornbrock. "We didn't say yea or nay on the candidate, but Mrs. Dornbrock said if I didn't vote for Corporate Susan she'd break my leg. I vote yes."

"I vote yes, also," said Bogdanovitch, "but from my own conviction."

"Yes," said Corporate Forziati. "I am surprised at the good judgment of the voters, but I vote yes with pleasure."

"Well I vote *no!* with pleasure!" said W. Guthrie Moore.

"It appears to be unanimous," said Cantrell. "The

next item on the agenda involves leasing space. . . ."
He paused. "Mr. Moore, there is no further business
that concerns you here. Leave or be thrown out."

After the Council meeting, Cantrell walked Marian
Yashon back to her office and sat down on her red
leather chaise longue.

"We have a problem, Tiger."

"What? You'd rather not lease space to G.Y. Fox,
Inc., for a ship-repair facility?"

"That's okay," he said. "I mean, God knows we have
plenty of space, and G.Y. Fox is the minority stockholder, after all. It's Corporate Susan Brown."

"What about her, Charles? Or it, if you'd rather."

"Frankly she scares the hell out of me. I tried to find
out why people were shooting at her, and she takes over
a place on the Council so I can't touch her no matter
what I find out. And look at the way she brutalized that
poor bastard Moore."

"Moore had it coming," said Marian.

"I quite agree," Cantrell said, "but how did it happen
that Corporate Susan knew how to push his buttons so
easily?"

"That's an interesting question," said Marian. "Off-
hand I'd say she'd been treating some of his ex-
girlfriends."

"That isn't very reassuring," he said. "What are we
going to do?"

"Nothing," said Marian. "The NAU is coming apart
at the seams. There is a revolution in Mexico and a
coup in St. Louis. Last I heard, the four generals had
shot the President and were taking over. When the dust
settles who's going to remember little old us?"

"It's not *us* that bothers me," said Cantrell. "Somebody has it in for Corporate Susan Brown. They won't
forget. After two nuclear attacks on Corporate Susan
I'm worried about a third. Innocent bystanders could
get seriously killed."

"How about French onion soup and a tossed salad?"
asked Marian, looking up from the luncheon menu.

"That sounds pretty good. You haven't answered my question."

"You asked the wrong question." She called the order in and turned in her chair to face him. "What you should have asked is what *can* we do?"

"All right then, Tiger, what *can* we do?"

"Start off by accepting that Corporate Susan Brown is here to stay. It will be easier to defend her than to get rid of her. Besides, she's a damned good doctor; you don't *want* to get rid of her."

"She draws nuclear bombs and we don't want to get rid of her?!"

"That's the down side, Charles. The up side is that we have the best health care in the Solar System."

"Jesus Christ, Marian! What good is it if we get blown to hell some fine morning?"

"Corporate Susan is treating my lower-back pain," said Marian. "What's left is intermittent and low grade. That nuclear attack you worry about may never happen, but I live with my back, and I used to live with the pain. You can say: for this you risk an atom bomb? I tell you that, at one point, to be free of the pain I was willing to risk a spinal operation!"

The serving cart rolled in, and they sat down beside it to eat lunch.

"Okay," said Cantrell, sprinkling grated Parmesan cheese on his soup. "If we're stuck with her, let's try to quantify the threat. Maybe it *is* too remote to worry about."

Marian finished her salad and picked up the desk phone. "Hey, Skaskash," she said, "I haven't been following events back home too closely. Would you give us an update on the general situation? Whatever happened to the four generals?"

"All dead," said Skaskash. "Their coup was ruthlessly quashed. Mexico *will* split. Cuba *may* split. Quebec is thinking about threatening to split. Bilingualism is out. Quotas are out. Old Time Religion is in. President Oysterman is the velvet glove, Willy Hulvey is the iron hand—"

"What's that about Hulvey?" asked Cantrell, the last spoonful of soup pausing in midair.

"On the record, William M. Hulvey, the Administrator of NAUGA-Security, has been named Acting Administrator for NAUGA-Army and -Navy," said Skaskash. "In the newspapers he has been variously described as a pillar, a bullyboy, a strongman, and a mainstay, but at the moment he seems to be in charge."

"Hulvey," said Cantrell. "Jesus Christ, what do we do now?"

"How about dessert?" asked Marian.

Late that evening Cantrell finally cleaned off his desk. "That will do for now," he said.

"Excuse me, Governor," said Skaskash with more deference than usual, "but I took the liberty of making an appointment for you to see Mrs. Wilhelmina Smith-Bakersfield."

"At 1930 hours?" The pain in Cantrell's voice would have touched the heart of a stone. Skaskash, however, was made of sterner stuff.

"Your schedule has been quite heavy today," said the robot. "I'd thought a busy man was always able to attend to one more detail. Perhaps you haven't been *that* busy?"

"Oh shut up. You want me to see Willie? That means I'll see her sooner or later. Put her on." Cantrell walked over to the telecon chair and sat down, blinking a little as the lights came on.

Mrs. Smith-Bakersfield materialized on the facing screen, her hair neatly coiffed, her hands folded, her dress primly gray.

"Thank you for making the time to see me, Charles," she said softly.

"It's always a pleasure to see you, Willie," replied Cantrell. "What's on your mind?"

"Franklin asked me to marry him," she said, "and I'd like you, yourself, to perform the ceremony."

"Of course," said Cantrell amiably. "I'd be delighted. Congratulations, or would it be best wishes? Who is Franklin?"

"Commander Franklin Stanton, NAUGA-Navy," she said, "former political officer on the *Ciudad Juárez*. You know him—he was counsel for defense at Major Terry's trial."

"Oh Christ," said Cantrell. "Yes, I do remember. We're still holding him and the other members of the political section for interrogation."

"That's *so* unnecessary," she said. "Franklin is a perfect gentleman; I'm sure he wouldn't hurt anyone. And if I married him, you could make me an officer of the court and remand him into my custody."

Cantrell looked at Skaskash. The face of Humphrey Bogart stared back at him, enigmatic, masklike. Skaskash showed his embarrassment by materializing a pair of sunglasses.

"I'll be very happy to tie the knot for the two of you, Willie, but there are a few things I have to work out with Skaskash first." Cantrell shook his head. "It may be a little while before we can turn your man Franklin loose."

Mrs. Smith-Bakersfield smiled at Cantrell with genuine warmth. It made her rather plain face look beautiful in a very special way, and he suddenly understood how Commander Stanton might be able to contemplate matrimony.

"Thank you so very, very much, Charles," she said. "I'm sure you'll be able to work things out for us in simply no time at all." She blew him a kiss and faded from the screen.

"Okay, Skaskash, tell me about it."

"There isn't much to tell, boss. Willie started visiting the prisoners to provide them with spiritual consolation, and she and Commander Stanton hit it off."

"Horseshit. She isn't a missionary, she's a missionary's widow. You put her up to it, didn't you?"

"Now why would I do a thing like that?"

"Spare me the sordid details; I don't want to know," said Cantrell. "You realize I don't dare turn Stanton loose, don't you?"

"Why not?" asked Skaskash.

"Because when he came in asking for Major Terry's life, I told him about my sons Willard and Charlie—I was reminding myself why I couldn't pardon Terry. But I told Stanton how Corporate Susan had screwed around with the genes and come up with better kids than Mishi and I would have done naturally—hell, *naturally* we might never have had kids at all. But Christ! Hulvey is trying to blow the hell out of Corporate Susan, and never mind the damn fools standing alongside, just because it has the capability to do genetic research on humans. Suppose he knew that *my* kids had been through the process? I don't know what he'd do, but I'd sure as hell hate to find out."

"You suspect he might be annoyed because you didn't have a license to conduct genetic research?" asked Skaskash.

"You could say that," replied Cantrell, "but considering what Hulvey has done when he *wasn't* annoyed, I don't want to—to provoke him."

"What about the wedding, then?"

"What about it? They can get married anytime they want; I just can't let Stanton loose afterward."

"At least not immediately," agreed the computer. "We could set up a nuptial suite in the prison compound and see that Willie gets all the conjugal visits she wants."

"And tell her it's an interim arrangement?"

"Ah . . . perhaps." Skaskash sounded doubtful.

"You suspect that the marriage might not take place if Stanton knew it wouldn't get him out of jail?"

"That is at least possible, boss. Perhaps if we double-crossed them?"

"Hey, Skaskash, are you looking to get rid of Willie?"

"She was helping me with my 'Meditations'—you know, the summa of my big theological work . . . and I find that she has become quite predictable."

"She bores you?"

The image of Humphrey Bogart nodded its head.

* * *

Later that week Charles Cantrell dropped in to see Commander McInterff, who had been recalled to active duty to command the NAUGA-Navy facility at Rosinante, a facility that had been authorized but never funded. McInterff was at his desk, working on the rigging of the USS *Constitution*.

"Wait until I finish tying this knot, and I'll be with you directly," he said. The line secured, he removed his jeweler's loupe and gave Cantrell a firm handshake.

"Sure, and it's a pleasure to be seeing you again, Governor. Now what is it that I might be doing for you?"

"I thought I might kick around a few ideas with you," said Cantrell. He looked over the office. "You have a bigger place than I do," he observed. "Of course the Navy is paying the rent."

"And my salary," said McInterff. "But as far as any hardware for the base is concerned, they have sent us never a penny."

"They may have had other things on their mind, Mac."

"I expect they had," agreed McInterff. "Can I give you to drink?"

"Coffee, please."

McInterff put water on to boil, and then took out a small jar of instant coffee and a cup. He opened the jar, removed the paper seal, and handed cup and jar to Cantrell.

"Help yourself, Governor," he said. "When the teakettle whistles, you'll be in business." He filled a shining nickel tea ball with Earl Grey and set it alongside the china teapot.

"Have you a spoon, Mac?"

"Only teaspoons," said McInterff, handing one over.

"That will do, thanks," said Cantrell. "You were, as I recall, in favor of supporting the L-4 Fleet when it mutinied. Do you still feel that way?"

"No, Governor, you did right to stand loyal. The way things broke, the Mexican Independence came about, and the restoration of the Old Regime—"

The teakettle whistled. McInterff filled Cantrell's cup and added a little boiling water to his teapot to take off the chill. He swirled the water around, dumped it, added the tea ball and finally fresh boiling water, setting his tea aside to steep.

"The Old Regime remains a dream for Celts and other romantics," he said. "The fat-arsed bureaucrats of the NAU have regrouped to uphold their grubby perks. Speaking of fat-arsed bureaucrats, incidentally, I got *this* yesterday."

He pulled the hard copy memorandum out of his In box.

"The Navy says they couldn't do anything about old 1848 because its code had been changed. They identify the new code as NIWRAD ARTNOC, which is one they claim not to have."

"Oh?" Cantrell took a sip of his coffee. "We found an encryption key in Joe Bob's briefcase. It wasn't identified, but I'll bet that's it! We could have turned the missile off from the beginning if we'd only known!"

"Maybe, maybe not. I doubt if there was any conspiracy involved, Governor," said McInterff, pouring a cup of tea and adding sugar and cream. "There's lots of leeway to explain things by ignorance and sloth, and in dealing with a bureaucracy, ignorance and sloth is surely the preferred explanation for just about anything."

"Did I mention the word 'conspiracy,' Mac? Surely I did not. But I will confess that my enthusiasm for that Navy base of yours is a trifle diminished."

"Don't you be doing anything rash," said McInterff. "I find it a great pleasure being paid to build these fine ship models in this magnificent office. You wouldn't want me to lose it for nothing, would you?"

"Do you give a damn?"

"No, Governor, I'd drop it for a real job in a minute—you know I would. But the Navy has nothing for me, and neither do you."

"Now that remains to be seen." Cantrell took another sip of coffee. "Suppose we are preparing to defend against a future missile attack, like the one just past. Have you any ideas? I mean it's a little late to be brainstorming once the missile is on its way."

Commander McInterff sat back for a while, drinking his tea.

"We might build a big laser," he said at last. "I mean a *really* big laser, Governor, say 50 meters by 10,000 meters, or even 20,000. Nothing ultra-hot like the Navy uses, but continuous, you know? Pump it with the big mirrors."

"Go on, Mac."

"Well, Governor, Navy weapons doctrine calls for a power source to generate light, the hotter the better. We have the big arrays of mirrors for light. No need to use a middleman, as it were. We just build a cool, continuous gas laser, but very, very big. It ought to have an effective range of maybe 200,000 kilometers, and it could pick off a missile like nothing, don't you know?"

"I like the idea, Mac. Can you do me a workup on it?"

"You're serious, Governor?"

"I don't know," said Cantrell, "this scratches an itch I seem to have developed."

"Well, in that case you ought to know that I got the idea from my drinking buddy, Harry Ilgen. He's a gun collector and a shop foreman for old Rubenstein. He had the thing worked out pretty good."

"I know Harry," Cantrell said. "Heavyset fellow with a crew cut?"

"That's him," agreed McInterff. "What do you think?"

Cantrell snapped open his belt phone. "Hey, Skaskash," he said, "has Henry Ilgen tried to sell you on a weapons project recently?"

"Yes," was the unhesitating reply, "a very large laser."

"What was wrong with it?"

"Nothing. He offered it as a defense against GNM 1848, only it couldn't be built in a timely fashion. The chemistry and physics were elegant, but the mechanical engineering needed work. Why do you ask?"

"Suddenly I find myself interested in such foolishness," said Cantrell. "I suppose I'm preparing to fight the last war, but I'd like to look over Ilgen's proposal."

"I'll have the hard copy on your desk when you get back," said Skaskash. "Do you want it costed?"

"Yes," said Cantrell, "we might just build the mother!"

CHAPTER 15

From: Captain Robert Lowell
Subject: Formal Reprimand
To: Executive Officer Luis Ruiz
Date: ————

(1) This reprimand is to be placed in your personnel folder as part of your permanent record.

(2) In accordance with my memorandum dated 28 May 41, it is the policy of the SS *Ciudad Juárez* to allow intership transfers within the L-4 Fleet without regard for the race or nationality of the transferees.

(3) The memorandum of 28 May 41 explicitly states that the performance level of the SS *Ciudad Juárez* is to be maintained or improved, that the levels of training and competence of the incoming transferees is of paramount importance, and that all transfers are to have my formal approval.

(4) These policy guidelines were followed without difficulty by your predecessor, Mr. Rogan, until the time of his own transfer.

(5) The recent transfer of 14 officers and men to the SS *Wyoming* fails to comply with the 28 May 41 memorandum on all the points cited in (2) and (3). (6) You are hereby relieved of all duties as Executive Officer on the SS *Ciudad Juárez.*

/s/

Robert Lowell, Captain

First Officer Antonio Jimenez read the hard copy of the reprimand and handed it back across the desk in the captain's cubbyhole of an office.

"I see you didn't date it," he said. "May one assume that you haven't formally signed it yet?"

"That is correct," said Lowell. "Will you take over the Executive Officer's duties until we can replace Mr. Ruiz? In addition to your own, of course."

"I think not, Captain," said Jimenez. "I am afraid it will be Luis that gets rid of *you*. The fourteen men he transferred out were the last Anglos on the ship. Except yourself, of course. I expect the replacements that Luis selected are partisans for Cuevas."

"I beg your pardon?" Lowell looked blank for a moment. "Who's he?"

"You've spent too much time with the internal politics of the L-4 Fleet," said Jimenez, shifting his weight in the straight-backed metal chair. "Pablo Cuevas is . . . well, he is Pablo Cuevas. He will lead the Republic of Mexico if he is not killed. If you had put your little reprimand on record, I think Luis would have had a good laugh. He would tell you to send it to Cuevas."

"One of the problems with having a mutiny is that it undermines the proper respect for authority," said Lowell. "It is very hard to maintain proper discipline afterward." He stood up and reached for the coffeepot. "Would you like a cup, Mr. Jimenez?" he asked.

"No, thank you, Captain."

Lowell poured himself a cup of coffee, and then felt the cup. He poured it back into the pot.

"Barely warm," he said. "The sensing element must

be out. If it were the heating element, the red light would have been out."

"We shall put it on the list for repairs," said Jimenez.

"Look," said Lowell earnestly, "if a reprimand won't do, how about throwing the son of a bitch in the brig?"

"You weren't listening, Captain," said Jimenez patiently. "On this ship, the balance of power has shifted to Luis. You are an able captain and a good man. I like you very much. But in a showdown with Luis I cannot help you."

Captain Lowell looked morosely at the empty coffee cup with its heeltap of cold coffee.

"I can't let the incident go by, Mr. Jimenez," he said at last. "What do you think I should do?"

"You ask my advice? I think you should stop worrying about the L-4 Fleet. They are too stupid to recognize good advice? Too bad. You can't make them take it. Give up also on this ship. It is not any God-given responsibility of yours. Like it or not, it will soon be part of the Mexican Navy. Look to yourself. What can you do for you?"

"I could transfer to the SS *Wyoming*."

"As what? Another staff officer? They have staff officers running out the ears. And none of the cruiser captains will want you aboard."

"I suppose not," Lowell agreed. "So I leave when I choose—or when Mr. Ruiz chooses—but where will I go?"

"Out of the L-4 Fleet, Captain Lowell," said Jimenez quietly. "You have played out your role in history. It was an honorable role and a necessary one, but now it is time to look for the bailing out."

Harry Ilgen stood before the blackboard he had covered with diagrams, beside the telecon screen that had displayed his slides, and behind the models he had set out for examination on the temporary Council table. He wiped his forehead with a red bandanna.

"That concludes my presentation," he said. "If the

honorable members of the Council have any questions, I shall be happy to try to answer them."

"What for do you need such an enormous laser?" asked Bogdanovitch.

"There are economies of scale—"

"No, Harry, that's why you designed it that way. I want to know what we *need* it for." He leaned on the table, which rocked slightly. "Who are we shooting at, Harry?"

"I don't know, Big John. *What* we are shooting at is any more missiles like old 1848 coming in this way. I don't know who'd be shooting them, but I don't know who shot off the first one, either."

"Do we really need such a big laser?" asked Corporate Forziati. "It seems to me that we could defend against a repeat of GNM 1848 with a somewhat smaller laser. Perhaps two orders of magnitude smaller, Mr. Ilgen. What do you need with all that extra capacity?"

"The big laser gives us a margin of safety," said Ilgen.

There was a long pause.

"Move the question," said Marian Yashon.

The vote was Dr. Yashon and Corporate Skaskash yes, Bogdanovitch, Dornbrock, and Corporate Forziati no.

"I am in favor of building a laser for defense," said Corporate Susan Brown. "I feel the threat as keenly as any of you. However, for this specific device my vote must be no.

"May I propose an alternate system, Mr. Chairman?"

"You have the floor, Dr. Brown," said Cantrell.

"Thank you." Corporate Susan faded from the screen to be replaced by a diagram.

"As you see, this is not any technical modification of what Mr. Ilgen presented us. It is, rather, a series of steps, with datelines, moving in the direction of the device that Mr. Ilgen would have us build.

"The first step is to build an experimental model

mounted on the mainframe here at Rosinante. We begin with five meters diameter rather than 200, a length of 230 meters rather than 23,000.

"It is not a weapon, but a step toward building the second large laser. We will gain engineering experience as we go along, and make changes, but I have suggested dimensions of 14 meters by 2,000. This is a formidable weapon, make no mistake. It would disable GNM 1848 at a range of 50,000 kilometers by *melting* it in 20 to 25 minutes."

"At which time it would be about 25,000 kilometers distant," said Dornbrock, "so you would have time to disable a second but not a third."

"I make that 35,000, so you could destroy a third but not a fourth," said Corporate Susan, "but your point is well taken. Concurrently with this work, we can proceed with the cleanup at Don Quixote. Yes, Mr. Bogdanovitch?"

"You project a target date of 1 September '41 for the cleanup. Where are you putting the stuff?"

"Following Mr. Dornbrock's suggestion, we are simply moving it around in orbit to park it by the abandoned works at Mundito Sancho Panza."

"We don't own Sancho Panza," said Corporate Forziati. "Such a move would constitute trespass, and we might lose our salvage rights."

"That may be true," said Corporate Skaskash, "but if we are successful in building the third stage being proposed up there, nobody is likely to argue with us."

"You simply project a third stage built by the Don Quixote mirror array," said Ilgen, "without any scale. How big do you think it would be?"

"I didn't make any estimate," replied Corporate Susan, "but the diameter would hardly be more than 30 or 40 meters. Your heat-transfer calculations are highly theoretical, and you have simply not addressed the problem of how to maintain an optically flat window 200 meters in diameter when the internal pressure is going to be on the order of 100 millibars with fluctuations of perhaps 200 percent."

"One advantage of the smaller device is that you might have a battery of three or more," said Skaskash. "If you used the double frustrum the way it's set up now, you might even put in two batteries."

Harry Ilgen folded his red bandanna and put it in his pants pocket.

"I would be delighted to go with Dr. Brown's proposal," he said. "It seems like an excellent way to proceed."

"Do you actually think the second stage will be operational by December 1?" said Cantrell.

"We will probably make the first trial run by then," said Corporate Susan. "I would think it would take three or four months before it could properly be called operational."

"It sounds good to me," said Bogdanovitch. "Move that we begin to build the laser system proposed by Mr. Ilgen following the steps outlined by Dr. Brown."

The motion passed unanimously.

"Come in please, the *George Ypsilanti Fox*," said Captain Robert Lowell. "This is the SS *Ciudad Juárez*." Lowell was cleanly shaved, and contrary to his recent practice, was wearing his freshly pressed class-A blues.

"Captain Schramm of the SS *Fox* here," came the reply. "What is it you want? We have clearance from your L-4 Fleet Command."

"We believe you may be moving contraband out of the L-4 zone," said Lowell blandly. "Please stand by to receive an inspecting party."

"We're headed for the asteroids," protested Schramm. "Your Command finally said we could go, and you people have never said what contraband *is*." He sighed. "Send your inspectors aboard."

"In this case, Captain Schramm, we believe you may have packed up the ship repair facility at Station Delta-3. We can hardly permit the movement of something so vital to the well-being of the L-4 Fleet, so it must be contraband." He smiled. "Your manifests say only 'used construction equipment.' I shall have to see for myself."

Captain Lowell turned to his first officer.

"Prepare the captain's gig, Mr. Jimenez," he said.

Jimenez saluted and left the bridge.

On the working deck he met with a group of ratings armed with pistols and Stangl rifles.

"Is the gringo ready to go?" asked Jimenez.

"Yes, sir," said Chief Petty Officer Estrelito. "His footlocker and wall locker are stowed under the air tanks in the gig's afterbay. His AWOL bag, too. I left his sidearm in the AWOL bag, as you ordered."

"Good. You know what to do next. Get moving and keep it quiet."

Jimenez returned to the bridge. "The gig is unshipped and ready for boarding, Captain," he said.

"Thank you, Mr. Jimenez," said Captain Lowell. "I shall debark at once."

Lowell keyed on the intercom. "Mr. Ruiz," he said. "Executive Officer Ruiz. Hey Luis! Come up on the bridge, Luis, I need to talk with you."

Lowell keyed off the intercom without waiting for an answer. He shook hands with Jimenez and left the bridge.

The gig was returning from the *SS Fox* before Executive Officer Luis Ruiz appeared on the bridge. He was not recently shaven or recently bathed. His fatigue uniform was out of press and unbuttoned. He carried a nonregulation .45 Colt revolver with pearl handles on his hip, and he was eating a doughnut.

Jimenez smiled, a mirthless baring of the teeth. He was half Apache, and sometimes it showed. It showed now.

"Mr. Ruiz," Jimenez said, "on the RMSS *Ciudad Juárez* I will not tolerate my officers looking a discredit to the Republic of Mexico!"

Ruiz, his mouth full of doughnut, gaped.

"The gringo put up with it," said Jimenez. "I am the captain now, and you are an unwashed, stinking slob and I will not have it!"

Ruiz swallowed his doughnut. "I am a lieutenant of Pablo Cuevas," said Ruiz, "and Cuevas is the rightful President of Mexico. If you don't like my style, that's too fucking bad!"

Off the bridge was the sound of a pistol shot. Ruiz turned, startled. He put his hand on his sidearm, then removed it very slowly as the two crewmen aimed 9mm service pistols at his chest.

"Take his sidearm before he shoots himself in the foot," said Jimenez.

One of the men stepped forward and lifted the .45 out of its holster.

From farther off came a burst of machine-gun fire, punctuated by the sharp crack of a Stangl rifle.

"When Pablo Cuevas becomes President, if he becomes President, he can make you Admiral and I will salute you, Mr. Ruiz," said Jimenez. "Until then, I am captain. You are disarmed, and your partisans will be disarmed shortly."

The intercom sounded.

"We took Rojas and six men prisoner," said CPO Estrelito. "One is a little wounded in the hand. Sanchez and ten others have locked themselves in the mess hall. One of them—Figueres, I think—is down in the hallway. Sanchez has a machine gun, and he says they have grenades. We lost Obregon and Kelly dead and two wounded, so far. Orders?"

"We have Mr. Ruiz," said Jimenez. "Perhaps he can persuade his men to surrender without further bloodshed."

Captain Jimenez turned to face Ruiz.

"Mr. Ruiz, would you be so kind as to request Mr. Sanchez and his little band to lay down their weapons and surrender?"

"And if I will not give such an order?" Ruiz said, staring defiantly at Antonio Jimenez, the Navy bureaucrat in the twenty-ninth year of an undistinguished career. An Apache warrior stared back at him.

"We will not even discuss such an unpleasant possibility," said Jimenez.

He keyed in the mess hall on the intercom.

"Now hear this! Now hear this!" he said. "This is Captain Jimenez. I have Mr. Ruiz with me. He has a few words to say to you."

"Viva Cuevas! Viva la Mexico!" came back the ragged shout.

"Go ahead, Luis," said Jimenez very softly.

There was a long pause.

"Who is in charge there?" came a voice from the intercom.

"Captain Jimenez," said Ruiz thickly. "He has taken this ship in the name of the Mexican Republic."

"Viva la Mexico!" said the intercom. "What about Cuevas, then, eh?"

"Mr. Sanchez, when Pablo Cuevas becomes President of Mexico he will make *you* the captain of this ship, if you live that long. Now it is Antonio Jimenez who is captain. Lay down your arms."

There was a heated discussion at the other end of the intercom.

"We will come out one at a time," said Sanchez, at last. "Tell your men not to shoot."

"Very good," said Captain Jimenez. He keyed in his CPO. "Mr. Estrelito, the men in the mess hall will surrender in a moment. Take any wounded to sick bay and lock the rest in number-five hold. Make sure the weapons are inventoried and locked up. Carry on."

"Yes, sir, Captain Jimenez," said CPO Estrelito. "Viva la Mexico! Viva Morales!"

Captain Jimenez turned to the second officer, who was seated in the con chair. "Has the gig been brought aboard yet, Mr. Velasquez?"

"It will be secured in a few minutes, Captain," said Velasquez.

"Good. When the gig is secured, set course for Station Delta-3."

"What for, Captain?" asked Velasquez. "All their equipment is going off on the SS *Fox*. They can make us no repairs."

"That's true," said Jimenez. "It is my intention to

put Mr. Ruiz and his men on the station as the Mexican garrison." He smiled, this time with a trace of humor. "Mr. Ruiz might even rename that hollow shell Station Pablo Cuevas. It would not seem inappropriate."

CHAPTER 16

On the afternoon of December 20, 2041, Governor Charles Cantrell was in his office, studying a model of a proposed sugar mill that would also provide fiber for paper or fiberboard as a by-product of sugar cane.

His phone rang.

"Governor Cantrell?" said a voice. "I am Captain Herbert O. Schramm of the SS *George Ypsilanti Fox*. The owner, Mr. Mason Fox, wishes to speak with you—" There was an indistinct voice in the background. "Well goddamnit, I'm not your secretary!" said Schramm away from the phone.

"Put Mr. Fox on, please," said Cantrell. Mason Fox was the chief executive officer of G.Y. Fox, Inc., and the chief minority stockholder of Rosinante, Inc., and he had for many years been Charles Cantrell's boss.

"Hello, there, Charlie, how have you been?" said Mason Fox.

"Pretty well, Mason," replied Cantrell. "What can I do for you?"

"Hey, Charlie, I'm on the SS *Fox*, and we have a little problem you can maybe help us with. The Jap cruiser *Higata* has said they're going to board us. We're about thirty-six hours out of Rosinante, and I expect the sons of bitches are going to haul off all our property. Your job: make 'em stop!"

"When are they boarding you?" asked Cantrell.

"In about an hour, I guess," said Mason. "They probably waited until we were this close to Rosinante so the lifeboats could make it in with no trouble. Very considerate of the thieving yellow bastards, God damn them!"

"I'll see what I can do for you, Mason," Cantrell said. "I used to deal with the Mitsui executives quite a bit, so maybe I can talk this lot around. Have Captain Schramm stand by, I may want him in a hurry."

"Charlie, I can't tell you how much I appreciate this. You don't know what it's been like, back in the L-4s, you just have no idea—"

"I'm going to be busy, Mason."

"Hey, Skaskash!" he yelled, "get me the range, relative velocity, acceleration and E.T.A. of the SS *Fox*!"

"Achtung! Achtung! Spitfeuer!" Skaskash manifested itself as Claude Raines, in a Luftwaffe flying officer's uniform, complete with a jaunty crushed cap and the Iron Cross, First Class. "The SS *Fox* is 110,000 kilometers distant, moving at 1,700 meters per second toward Rosinante, accelerating at -0.0135 centimeters per second per second. Estimated arrival time is December 22, 2041, at 0215 hours, unless the INSS *Higata* gets to her first."

"How soon?"

"Fifty-five-point-two minutes," said Skaskash.

"Okay," said Cantrell, "get me the data on the *Higata* out of *Jane's Fighting Ships*. Hard copy, please."

He snapped open his belt phone and pushed the button for Marian.

"Are you still up at Harry Ilgen's shop?" he asked.

"Yes, but we're almost finished. What's up?"

Cantrell told her.

"Okay," said Marian, "the 4.6-meter laser is operational, but not too powerful. The modified configuration on the 14.2-meter laser is complete, but Ilgen is still checking out the controls. They figured to have the test firing done by 1700 hours."

"I'll give them fifteen minutes," said Cantrell.

"You'll have it," said Marian.

"Aye canna promise a thing, Cap'n," came Ilgen's voice in the background.

"Fine," said Cantrell, "I want both lasers tracking the INSS *Higata*, and I want them both warmed up, ready to go . . . Skaskash, put a call through to the *Higata*."

"*Jawohl, mein Kapitan!*"

"And Skaskash—I want the status of the two lasers on the telecon screen."

"*Jawohl, mein Führer!*"

"And have Captain Schramm on the SS *Fox* give us the temperature readings on the *Higata*'s radiators. He can see them and we can't. I want those on the telecon screen, too."

"*Ja, ja, Herr Oberst.*" Skaskash gave the military salute and vanished.

The telecon screen now displayed the schematic diagram of the INSS *Higata*, a red oval, and the SS *Fox*, a green circle. The numbers, periodically revised, floated alongside the markers. The laser status report appeared in the lower left-hand corner of the screen. Yellow letters said: 4.6 READY 100, 14.2 READY 70. In the lower right-hand corner yellow letters said: HIGATA RAD. TEMP. 225°C.

Cantrell's desk pushed up a hard copy of the information in *Jane's* on the INSS *Higata*.

"Well," said Cantrell, "it's about time."

"I've been busy," said the disembodied voice of Skaskash. "Marian has me working the mirrors."

"Can you manage?" asked Cantrell.

"Oh, hell yes," was the reply, "I can modulate those laser beams so they play 'Dixie' if Ilgen will just get on the stick with the 14.2."

In the lower left hand corner of the screen: 14.2 READY 70 changed to 14.2 READY 80.

Cantrell looked at the information on the *Higata*. Range, size, speed, crew, armor, he passed over quickly, but armament—the *Higata* carried six 100-kiloton GNMs. Cantrell grimaced.

"Captain Bunjiro Norigawa of the INSS *Higata* will speak with you in a few seconds," said Skaskash. "Better get on the telecon seat."

"I'm in it," said Cantrell. He snapped open his belt phone. "Marian, I'll give firing commands over this line. Float any answers or questions across the top of the screen, okay?"

"No problem," she said, and NO PROBLEM floated across the top of the screen in luminous purple letters.

Then the face of Captain Norigawa appeared on the screen. He was a balding man with close-cropped hair gray at the temples and a deeply lined face. He was perhaps fifty years old, and wore the dress whites of the Imperial Japanese Navy. He sat patiently, waiting for Cantrell to speak.

"I am Charles Chavez Cantrell, Governor of Mundito Rosinante," said Cantrell formally. "When has it become the policy of the Imperial Japanese Navy to engage in acts of piracy?"

"Bunjiro Norigawa, captain of the INSS *Higata*," replied Norigawa, with a slight bow. "There can be no question of piracy in this case, since I am acting in strict obedience to the orders of my Government."

Cantrell returned the bow.

"Theft is theft," he said. "I must ask you not to interfere with the SS *Fox*."

"Property is an interesting concept," said Norigawa. "In essence, the State agrees to enforce your claim to a given item in return for your taxes. When the State is unable to enforce your claim, the property right exists only to the extent that you yourself are able to enforce it. It is my intention to intercept the SS *Fox* and its cargo."

In the lower left-hand corner of the screen, yellow letters said: 4.6 READY 100, 14.2 READY 80. The 14.2

READY 80 began to blink, and changed to 14.2 READY 90.

"That is most unfortunate," said Cantrell. "If I cannot dissuade you from this act of piracy, then I must destroy your ship."

"So sorry, Governor Cantrell," replied Norigawa, "there is no piracy involved. And I am fully aware of the capabilities of the Mitsubishi Dragon Scale Mirror. Our present course will not take us within 10,000 kilometers of it, far beyond its effective range."

In the lower left-hand corner, 14.2 READY 90 remained unchanged.

"Would you prefer to describe it as an act of undeclared war?" asked Cantrell. "Piracy is colorful, shorter, and precisely descriptive."

"An act of undeclared war looks much better when written up in one's personnel folder," said Norigawa. "However, it is pointless to continue this discussion any further. With your permission, I should like to attend to my shipboard duties."

Cantrell snapped open his belt phone.

"Hit him with the 4.6-meter laser," he said.

4.6 ON TARGET AND FIRING, said purple letters floating across the screen.

"I am very sorry, Captain Norigawa," said Cantrell, "but we have acquired the technical means to extend the range of our mirror array. We are now using the minimum applicable force, and if it is insufficient, we will increase it as much as is necessary. . . . I would be honored if you would join me in a cup of coffee, however."

Bunjiro spoke to someone off camera. Presently he sat facing Cantrell over a cup of tea, while Cantrell's receptionist served him a cup of coffee.

After a while the lower right-hand corner of the screen started flashing.

Higata Rad. Temp. went from 225 to 226°C.

On the other side, 14.2 READY 90 remained unchanged.

"I am informed that you are directing some sort of

heat ray at the *Higata*," said Bunjiro calmly. "I offer my congratulations on your ingenuity."

"Thank you," said Cantrell. "You are not as yet persuaded that it is any threat to the *Higata*?"

"Unfortunately, no," said Norigawa. "It remains my intention to carry out my orders."

Higata Rad. Temp. remained at 226°C.

The lower left-hand corner of the screen began flashing.

The 14.2 READY 90 changed to 14.2 READY 100.

Cantrell snapped open his belt phone. "Give me 50-percent output on the 14.2 meter laser," he said.

14.2 ON TARGET AND FIRING AT 50 PERCENT, said the purple letters.

Outside, the sky became dark, as if some great cloud passed over the sun while Skaskash diverted the mirrors from providing sunlight to the 14.2-meter laser.

"Do we have enough mirror capacity?" Cantrell asked.

YES, said the purple letters, THE OPTICAL SURFACE OF THE LASER IS DESIGNED TO DEFORM INTO ITS PROPER CONFIGURATION AT FULL OPERATION. WE ARE APPLYING 98.9 PERCENT OF THE PUMPING INPUT AND GETTING . . . OH, SAY 47 OR 48 PERCENT POWER PUT OUT. A different typeface appeared, floating across the top of the screen.

THIS IS ILGEN, said the gothic letters. THE GOD-DAMNED OPTICAL FACE ISN'T STABLE! IF WE DON'T RE-DUCE THE INPUT, IT'S GOING TO DRIFT UPWARD AS IT STARTS TO HEAT UP.

Higata Rad. Temp. went from 228 to 229°C.

Cantrell sipped his coffee.

Higata Rad. Temp. went from 230 to 231°C.

"Governor Cantrell, I must request that you turn off your heat ray," said Bunjiro. "If you do not, I will be compelled to destroy Mundito Rosinante with missile fire."

WE CUT THE PUMPING INPUT TO 96.0 PERCENT, said the gothic letters, THE OUTPUT IS UP AROUND 52 OR 53 PERCENT.

Higata Rad. Temp. went from 234 to 235°C.

"I regret that that is impossible," said Cantrell, displaying a calm he did not feel. "The device we are using against the *Higata* was designed as a defense against missiles. We can destroy your missiles in flight, and such a demonstration of implacable hostility on your part would necessitate the regrettable destruction of the INSS *Higata*."

THE SEAL AROUND THE OPTICAL SURFACE IS STARTING TO CRACK, said the purple letters, INPUT 90 PERCENT, OUTPUT 58 to 60 PERCENT.

Cantrell took a sip of coffee.

Higata Rad. Temp. went from 249 to 250°C.

"Turn off your heat ray immediately!" said Norigawa.

"Perhaps you wish to consult your Admiralty," suggested Cantrell.

"No! I do not wish to report failure!"

Higata Rad. Temp. went from 254 to 256°C.

"May I suggest that you have obtained information of far more value to the Imperial Navy than any cargo of second-hand machinery, Captain Norigawa?" Cantrell said politely. "The use of very-large-scale lasers in conjunction with the Mitsubishi Dragon Scale Mirror must surely be of profound interest to your Government!"

Higata Rad. Temp. went from 266 to 268°C.

MORE CRACKS, said the purple letters. LOOKS LIKE LEAKAGE, TOO. OUTPUT DOWN TO 54 PERCENT, INPUT AT 60 PERCENT.

"Prepare to load missiles!" shouted Captain Norigawa.

"Stop closing with the SS *Fox*," barked Cantrell, "or I'll raise the power to 100 percent!"

"Alter course away from SS *Fox*," said Norigawa to someone off camera.

Higata Rad. Temp. went from 280 to 282°C.

"Divert laser beam from *Higata*!" said Cantrell into his belt phone.

JAWOHL, HERR OBERST! said the purple letters.

WE SEEM TO BE LOSING GAS RATHER FAST, said the gothic letters. I DOUBT IF YOU'LL GET ANY MORE MILEAGE OUT OF THIS ONE TODAY.

"Cool off laser, slowly," said Cantrell into his belt phone, "but please stand by."

YOU'VE GOT TO BE TALKING TO THE JAP, said the gothic letters. WE HAVE A TWO-METER CRACK SPREADING OUT ACROSS THE OPTICAL FACE!

"Captain Norigawa, I am profoundly gratified that we have been able to resolve this business in such a reasonable and equitable manner. Your present course will bring you to Mundito Rosinante in about thirty-six hours. I would be most honored if you would be my guest at dinner."

"The honor would be mine," said Bunjiro Norigawa formally.

The laser control room looked like the inside of a breadboarded black box, clutter piled upon random junk in great disorderly stacks. But how the data poured in! Data on temperature, pressure, geometry, the data on the-energy-content-of-the-beam-at-the-*Higata.* Correlated data, compiled data, sublime and effervescently giddy data. The experiment was over, and now the fun was about to begin again.

"Fourteen-point-two meters is *definitely* too big," said Harry Ilgen, "but the hexagonal array kept the optical surfaces flat, all right."

"We can make the hexagonal elements out of silica," said Skaskash, "and arrange those elements as a spherical surface to support the pressure, while the optically flat plate set into each element remains set at the precise angle! . . ."

"We're having a formal dinner, Charles?" said Marian into her purse phone. "You mean a formal *Japanese* dinner? Charles, what am I going to wear?!"

"Yes! Yes!" said Ilgen. "If we make the tube 12 meters, or 12.5 max, we can use a segment of a sphere—oh, say 15 meters in diameter for the window."

"We can go 12.5 for the mirror," said S askash, "but it needn't bear a load to deform it—we can make the tube 12.65. What about your idea to maximize the light density by using only one of the three colors of light our mirrors reflect?"

"Well, how many people are there going to be?" asked Marian. "Look, Charles, this is *serious*! Okay, we'll go with the Council and call it a State dinner, and that has got to be it. Seven of us, seven of them. And I still don't have anything to wear."

"We've worked out the system for the green light best," said Ilgen, running his hand over his crew cut. "We have that stack of mirrors—the red and blue mirrors left over from the quality-control work on making the big array—could we use them? How many do we have?"

"The red and blue combined? Maybe 60 or 70 hectares," said Skaskash. "That would give us a working length of maybe 16 kilometers. I think we really need 21 or 22."

"Yes, 22 would take all the green light from one of the frustrums on the Don Q array—if we patched it up. But what about the cooling?"

"So long, Harry, I'm heading back to the office," said Marian, pausing at the door. Harry Ilgen didn't look up.

"Bye-bye," he said. "Hey! Skaskash! If we built a pressurized jacket, oh, say one kilometer in diameter, the laser would be *air*-cooled except for the face, which would be silica! Then we could run a higher light-density and 16 kilometers would be enough! Hell! We could do it with 10!"

Skaskash began generating the proposed design, with Ilgen making suggestions and marking up the drawing with a light pencil.

They built a pavilion on the lawn outside Cantrell's office, using steel and glass and aluminum, lavishly overlaid with wood-grain adhesive vinyl. A stairway, of black painted steel, ran from Cantrell's balcony to the deck of the pavilion. *Shoji*—translucent sliding panels—edged the pavilion proper and replaced the French doors on the balcony.

A large order of fireworks was placed with Mordecai Rubenstein.

A dozen flowering cherry trees were placed in large pots and moved, via drop ship, to the pavilion garden. The manager of the cherry orchard took a dim view of such foolishness, but conceded that his trees had been well handled.

A hole was cut in the wall to provide direct access to the Executive Dining Room kitchen.

A call went out for koto players and sake servers.

A call went out for sake.

Cantrell practiced his conversational Japanese with his wife, Mishi.

Skaskash brushed up on Japanese movies, as late as 2006, the end of the postrenaissance efflorescence.

Marian discovered the soft brown pants suit she'd pushed to the back of the closet as being too nice to wear to the office. She decided that if she wore it with her cream-colored silk blouse, the dinner might come off after all.

Captain Norigawa, looking at the invitation to join Governor Cantrell and the Council of Rosinante at dinner, had his Executive Officer inquire how many were on the Council. The Executive Officer reported back, correctly, that there were seven.

Norigawa then informed Cantrell's office that he and seven officers would be arriving for dinner on December 23, at 1900 hours.

At 1530 hours on December 23, Cantrell said, "Norigawa will lose face if we only have seven people on our side of the table; we need to invite an eighth person."

"It should be someone with a bit of importance," said Marian, "with a bit of class, if possible. Maybe Skaskash could do an impersonation."

"No more telecon screens at the dinner table," said Cantrell. "What about Commander McInterff?"

"When he gets a few under his belt he starts talking about the Old Regime," said Marian. "We'd be better off without him. What about your old boss, Mason Fox?"

Cantrell snapped his phone open. "Hello, Mason. Cantrell here. Look, this is kind of short notice, but can you make it over for a formal dinner tonight?"

"You mean for the Jap captain? Hey, Charlie, I'm afraid I'm kind of busy tonight. My advance people screwed up—you know? Tell you what, though. I've got a fellow here I can send over. My Naval Procurement Consultant—he's more decorative than useful. Mr. Lovell. Okay?"

"He'll do," said Cantrell. "Tell him business-suit formal. He can call my office for a private trolly to pick him up. Thanks, Mason."

Cantrell's receptionist, Mrs. Omi Smith, came in. She was smiling.

"Please, Mr. Cantrell, sir, I made these ties for the dinner. I would be honored if you would deign to wear one." She held out a box containing four ties of green silk the exact shade of the Rosinante logo. The logo, a rickety green horse on a white field, appeared as a disk of white embroidered silk within a thin white circle. Within the disk was the green horse, the whole thing about two centimeters in diameter.

Cantrell picked up one of the ties. It was fully lined and sensuously soft to the hand.

"I will be most pleased to wear this," he said. "You might also approach Mr. Dornbrock and Mr. Bogdanovitch." He smiled very faintly. "As good Union men they may not choose to wear the company tie."

The receptionist giggled. "Oh, no, Mr. Cantrell, this is not *company* tie, this is *Rosinante* tie."

Dornbrock and Bogdanovitch evidently thought so, too. Both wore the tie, Dornbrock with his double-breasted brown pinstripe suit, Bogdanovitch with a blue blazer and gray slacks.

Cantrell wore his dark gray suit and a white shirt. The green tie looked very dashing.

The private trolly he had sent around for Norigawa and his officers arrived in front of the lobby at precisely 1900 hours.

There was a ninth person with them, an Occidental wearing a dark gray suit, with a white shirt and the green Rosinante tie.

"That must be Mr. Lovell," said Marian.

"My God!" said Cantrell. "It's Captain Robert Lowell!"

"He *can't* be at our party," said Marian, "*do* something!"

Then Cantrell was shaking hands and being introduced to Norigawa's officers.

"I have a favor to ask of you, Governor Cantrell," Norigawa said. "On the trolly ride over, I had a most enjoyable conversation with Captain Lowell here. Would it be possible to arrange the seating so that it might continue?"

"I don't really know . . ." said Cantrell, looking at Marian.

"We were going to put you on the end, opposite Charles, here," she said, "but if we put you in the middle, you can still be opposite Charles, and we can seat Captain Lowell on Charles's left. Will that be satisfactory?"

"Yes, please," said Captain Norigawa. "Thank you so much."

Moving from right to left on the Rosinante side of the table were Corporate Forziati, wearing a dark gray suit and the Rosinante tie; Corporate Susan Brown, wearing a green silk kimono, seemingly made of the same material as the tie, and marked with the Rosinante logo; Marian, who wore the Rosinante logo on an emerald-and-platinum pin given her by Mordecai Rubenstein; Cantrell, Lowell, and Skaskash, manifesting itself as Toshiro Mifune in a dark gray suit and the Rosinante tie. At the end of the table were Dornbrock and Bogdanovitch.

It was an incredibly good party.

Skaskash conversed in fluent Japanese—with English subtitles on his telecon screens (two small ones at right angles for the people on his side of the table) to the great amusement of the Japanese officers who all read English. Skaskash also provided simultaneous translation for the non-Japanese-speaking members of the party, Marian, Dornbrock, and Bogdanovitch.

A notable thing: the maid pouring sake would walk behind Skaskash's telecon screen and pause. *On* the telecon screen she would appear as smoothly synchronized with her real self as you could wish, and the image of the maid would kneel beside the image of Skaskash and pour the image of sake into the image of his cup. Then the image of the maid would walk off the telecon screen as the maid, on cue, would reappear.

There were numerous highlights.

The haiku contest produced both beautiful and witty haiku, as Skaskash and Susan Brown inspired Bunjiro's officers.

The soup—mussels and scallions with rice noodles—provided an opportunity for soup-slurping. Cantrell, being Occidental, did not compete. He was already familiar with the catch-22 involved; if he didn't slurp soup he was a barbarian, and if he did, he hadn't been properly brought up.

Skaskash, however, slurped his soup with electronic amplification, amazing even himself, until he fished a microphone out of the liquid with chopsticks, and demonstrated that it was live by tapping it against the side of the bowl.

Over the main course, an excellent lobster salad, Captain Lowell held the company spellbound with his account of the L-4 Mutiny.

Afterward, Skaskash and Susan Brown sang the love duet from *Madame Butterfly* and as an encore Susan Brown gave the company "One Fine Day." Both computers were profound students of human nature, and both were fully in control of their vocal apparatus. Performed at La Scala, the duet would have started a riot because of Skaskash's interpretation of Toshiro Mifune's interpretation of Pinkerton. The final number would have redeemed a mediocre performance, and capping a good one would have had the house on its feet cheering for twenty minutes.

When the applause at dinner died down, the *shoji* were opened to show the cherry blossoms in the moonlight. Skaskash, artfully manipulating the mirrors, produced the illusion of dark sky and luminous clouds with a swollen yellow moon rising above the horizon.

Captain Norigawa and Governor Cantrell ended the evening standing at the head of the stairs outside Cantrell's office, watching the fireworks.

"Beautiful," said Norigawa, watching the gold and orange and green explosions swell and cascade downward. "You do things so exquisitely well, here in Rosinante. If you should decide to declare your independence from the warring factions of the NAU, you may rest assured of Japan's support."

The next morning Cantrell saw Norigawa and his officers to the express elevator transfer station. The band played, a tenor sang, supported by a soldiers' chorus, and an honor guard passed in review. Cantrell noted that the flags displayed were the green horse of Rosinante, the Stars and Bars of the old Confederacy, the State Flag of Texas, and the Stars and Stripes of the Old Regime. The North American Union's flag remained cased, paraded in the place of honor, but not displayed.

Norigawa, saluting as the flags passed before him, showed not the slightest sign that he noticed anything unusual.

Cantrell passed his hand over the back of his neck, trying to make the hair lie down.

As Captain Bunjiro Norigawa was about to enter the elevator, Cantrell handed him two 8-by-13-centimeter digital recordings.

"Skaskash tells me that you asked for a tape of last night's performances," he said. "He begs you to accept these."

"Thank you so much, Governor Cantrell."

"He also asked me to give you this," Cantrell said, handing Norigawa a slim book, printed in Japanese.

"He told me that it was a summary of his four-volume work on religion."

"Your vassal displays amazing talents. Please thank him on my behalf." He turned the little book over in his hands. "*Meditations on Life in Space*. The character Skaskash uses for space also means emptiness." Norigawa leafed through the book. "Did he do his own calligraphy? Yes, I see he has endorsed the book. Beautiful. His calligraphy is beautiful. I shall read it with great attention, I promise."

Norigawa bowed. Cantrell returned the bow.

"Thank you so much," said Norigawa.

"You do me too much honor," said Cantrell.

Then the elevator doors closed, and the Japanese Navy departed.

"Vassal?" said Cantrell.

On January 2, 2042, Commander McInterff requested an appointment with Governor Cantrell.

Formally.

"Very unlike McInterff," said Cantrell. "I wonder what he wants?"

"We'll see," said Marian, drawing herself a cup of coffee. "Are you going to remove the pavilion?"

"I don't know. We sent the cherry trees back, but the pavilion is kind of fun. I will have the French doors replaced, though."

"Commander McInterff to see you, sir," said the receptionist.

"He's right on time. Send him in."

McInterff entered, long-faced and wearing his class-A blues.

"Good morning, Governor Cantrell. I have received instructions from my Government to arrest Captain Robert Lowell and to arrange for his transportation to Laputa to stand trial on charges of treason. My instructions acknowledge that I have no means to enforce this order except my own right arm, and they explicitly say that I am to ask for your cooperation."

"How long have you had the order?" asked Marian.

"Since Christmas Day," replied McInterff. "I pretended I was on vacation and didn't see the evil thing. Nothing that I had to do as a ship's engineer ever grieved me half as much, and I daren't refuse the order. Hulvey himself was the one who signed it."

"Let's consider our options," said Marian, taking a sip of coffee. "There are probably several things we can do."

"We don't have any options," said Cantrell. "I know *what* we have to do, the only question is *how*."

CHAPTER 17

Mist and darkness. Hulvey stood on a cobblestone path beside a dark, slowly moving river. His breath made a persistent cloud in the cold, damp air, and the vapor rising from the river obscured the windowless warehouses on either side. Before him was a low-arched stone bridge, blackness beneath, the haloed light of a single street lamp casting a feeble glow above.

The body of Joe Bob Baroody, face bloody, his right arm blown away, drifted out of the darkness under the bridge and dissolved into the mist. Terrified, Hulvey was unable to move.

He heard a man crying. The mist parted to show Stanley Bowman, lying on a couch and weeping at the knowledge of his impending doom. Hulvey tried to call out to him, but no sound came. He turned his face away, and Bowman vanished.

His son, Riordan, dressed as he had been on the

fishing trip after graduating from the Havana Missile School, walked soundlessly out of the darkness, his tanned face unsmiling.

"I have assumed command of the NAUSS *Vancouver*," said Riordan. "Father, I love you." He saluted.

Hulvey tried to return the salute and could not. He tried to reach out to his son and could not move. He tried to speak and no sound came.

Riordan dissolved into the mist.

There was a faint, familiar, terrifying odor of antiseptic. A little girl in a print dress ran before him, crying, "Don't hurt Jennie! Don't hurt Jennie!"

Out of the mist a figure appeared, walking haltingly on crippled feet.

Dolores Ferranes knelt awkwardly and with crippled hands embraced the little girl.

"Don't cry, honey," she said, "he wouldn't listen to me, either. Good-bye, Willy."

Dolores shouldn't be here, Hulvey thought, not Dolores.

"Dolores," he cried thickly, "Dolores, what shall I do?"

The sound of his own voice woke him.

He sat up and looked at his bedside clock. The time was 0208. The outside temperature was -25°C. The big cold front they had been talking about must have arrived.

He put on his old blue bathrobe and went into the kitchen to brew a pot of tea.

While the tea was steeping, Corporate Elna interrupted him.

"Excuse me. Dr. Khonev at the hospital is on the line. Dolores had a cardiac arrest about half an hour ago. They are preparing to attempt to revive her, but Khonev feels there has been brain damage. He wishes to know if he should proceed, anyway."

"No," said Hulvey. "Dolores is gone. Tell him not to bother."

Presently he poured himself a cup of tea out of the yellow melamine teapot.

"If I had tears, then would I shed them now," he said. "I always told her she smoked too much."

"Excuse me," said Elna, "I didn't catch the last phrase."

There was a long silence.

"Has anything turned up at the office?"

"The Reverend Daugherty has invited you to appear on his show to explain why you have fallen from the faith lately."

"Christ!" growled Hulvey. "I'm reorganizing the fucking Government in the middle of a fucking revolution and *he* wants to know why 'you have fallen from the faith lately.' " He took a sip of tea. "Poor Daugherty. With the Hispanic Catholics gone, the Fundamentalist majority is down the tubes, and he can't change. Say no, but politely. What else?"

"We have a response from Governor Cantrell on our request for the extradition of Captain Robert Lowell."

"Oh? He wouldn't move when we asked nicely. What does he say now?"

"A waffle," said the computer. "He talks about anti-hegemonism and states' rights and doesn't say anything exactly."

"Send it over to Legal to process as expeditiously as possible. I want that son of a bitch Lowell nailed to the wall. Go on."

"There is a message directed to you, personally, from Laputa," said the computer. "It is written in the NI-WRAD ARTNOC encryption key."

Hulvey sat in silence for a moment, watching the fragrant steam rise from his teacup.

"Simon says: you have my permission to remember the location of the encryption key," he said.

"Yes," said Corporate Elna.

"Simon says: you have my permission to translate the message."

"Yes," said Corporate Elna. "One minute, please."

Hulvey sat and drank his tea.

"Ready," said Corporate Elna.

"You may print me a hard copy of the translation,"

said Hulvey. If he had prefaced his order with "Simon says," the computer would have erased the translation and put the encryption key under a forty-eight-hour time lock.

Hulvey pushed his chair back and reached over to take the hard copy from his kitchen printer.

Dear Mr. Hulvey:

Having never had the honor of your direct acquaintance, I am unaware of what I have done to earn your enmity. In the last two years, however, that enmity has been far from the least of my burdens.

I will not return Captain Robert Lowell to you for judgment under any circumstances whatsoever.

If this means war, and the severance of the ties that bind Rosinante to the North American Union, so be it. The choice is yours.

I appeal to your sense of honor, your sense of justice, and your sense of the national interest to override the perverse and malicious motives that have inspired your vendetta against me.

> Charles Chavez Cantrell
> Governor of Rosinante

"He must have used Joe Bob's encryption key," Hulvey said at last, "and he found out the name of the key from the Navy. And sending the message to me wasn't too hard a guess to make."

He refilled his teacup.

"I see he doesn't mention Corporate Susan Brown at all. Well, there's no help for it. 'Now I have waded so far deep in gore, the way were as long back as on before.' "

"You've been hitting the classics again," said Corporate Elna. "Was that Poul Anderson?"

"Shakespeare," said Hulvey, "from *Macbeth*. Maybe Anderson used the quote somewhere."

He sat in the kitchen working on routine business until the sun rose.

CHAPTER 18

The office of Triple Administrator William M. Hulvey was furnished with genuine antiques loaned by museums and private collections. The criterion for selection was whether or not a given item had increased sharply in value in the last decade. Gilt bronze kitsch had appreciated heavily in that time, and gilt bronze kitsch provided what unity of concept there was. Since Hulvey's office was frequently publicized, the value of the displayed items went up even further, allowing the museums and collectors who lent them to count a kind of kitschy coup.

The Administrator sat in live conference with Fleet Admiral Nguen Tran Vong, and Vong's Chief of Technical Operations Staff, Captain Elaine Chen.

"I am profoundly embarrassed," said Vong. "I felt as you did, that Cantrell's threat to withdraw from the NAU was a bluff." He did not look embarrassed. In private he had argued that Cantrell was not bluffing. "After the event, I asked myself why? After the event, I ordered high-resolution pictures taken from Laputa. Captain Chen will show you what we found."

Elaine Chen took a folder of glossy prints from her briefcase and laid it on the table before her.

"This is the double frustum of Don Quixote during the cleanup," she said, turning the print over. "This is almost the same view taken on January 20, showing the construction in the right-hand frustum in the interim. The technicians call it the Purple Shaft. Notice the support system, which can rotate the shaft in two planes. I imagine that if it was aimed at an object on the other side of the mirror array, a few of the mirrors could be removed."

She turned the print over.

"This is an enlarged view of the same scene. It shows the Purple Shaft very clearly. We estimate that it is 1020 meters in diameter, 17,230 meters long. The outer surface is made of salvaged purlin tile mounted in salvaged purlin frames. The faint diamond pattern shows quite clearly."

"It doesn't look purple at all," said Hulvey. "Why do they call it the Purple Shaft?"

Captain Chen turned the print over.

"This is the device in operation," she said. "A very short exposure time shows the inner structure vividly. It is a tube twelve or thirteen meters in diameter running the length of the structure. It is evidently covered with red and blue layered mirrors, so that it reflects purple light and passes green light into the gas mixture which the inner tube contains. In effect, you are looking at a huge gas laser pumped by an array of mirrors having an area of thousands of square kilometers."

"What's in the gas mixture?" asked Hulvey.

"The radiation data is consistent with methyl isopropyl mercury and carbon dioxide," she replied, "but we don't know." She turned the print over. "This is a somewhat longer exposure. The envelope glows with reflected purple light, and you can't see the inner structure at all, except for the optical window at the end . . . the little white spot, there. From the color, the temperature of the window must be about 1,100°C, and it is probably made of silica. It is almost certainly made of silica."

"Is it using the full power of the mirror array?" Hulvey asked.

"No, on that shot they were using 30 percent," she said. "We took a picture of the mirror, and had the computer calculate the angle of each mirror in the array. It gave us a false-color developed picture." She pulled a print out of the pile. "Yellow is aimed at the laser, the red and red-purple are not. The little green rectangle was probably being used for something else."

"Could they use the full power of the array to pump the laser?" asked Admiral Vong.

"They've had it as high as 80 percent," she said. "That is, we've seen them take it as high as 80 percent. It is a formidable weapon."

"Would you say that it is sufficient to enforce their separation from the NAU?" asked Hulvey.

"Cantrell evidently thinks so," said Vong. "We could probably destroy Rosinante with a salvo of thirty or forty missiles, but I doubt if we have the will to proceed in such a bloody fashion."

"Do you now?" said Hulvey. "Are you trying to make policy for me again, Nguen?"

"No sir," said Vong. "However, the two Mexicos and Cuba might not feel that such a harsh response to secession was justified." He looked into Hulvey's eyes. "Neither would I."

"Excuse me," said Corporate Elna. "The Japanese have formally recognized Rosinante as an independent nation."

"Neither would the Japanese," said Vong.

"Perhaps not," said Hulvey. "When did *that* happen?"

"This morning," said Elna. "It came over JapaNews as an official bulletin."

"Ah, so," said Hulvey. He walked over to the window and stood looking out over the courtyard for a while. A very fine snow was falling.

"A hypothetical question, Admiral Vong," he said at last. "When would be the earliest you could move against Rosinante?"

"Not before we deal with the Old Regimist fleetshard in the L-4s. We're still putting the L-5 Fleet back in shape . . . so say we move in March. Our target date is March 1. The best case is the Old Regimists see us coming and don't fight. They turn the ships over to the Mexicans and take sanctuary in the U.S. of M. If they fight, we'll wipe them out, but we'll take some damage, some casualties. Afterward, you want to send a squadron out to Rosinante." Admiral Nguen Tran Vong hesitated. "Assuming you are willing to spare one, they could be under way by March 15—April 1 if there was fighting."

"And if we wished to conceal the reason for sending out such a force?"

"We would say they were en route to Ceres," said Vong. "We should have sent reinforcements to Ceres a long time ago, and Rosinante is hardly out of the way for such a move."

"I remember," said Hulvey, "the Japanese have been giving us trouble out there. We really should do something about that." He nodded his head. "We really should."

In deference to Grand Admiral Shinaka, the Supreme Commander of the Imperial Navy of Japan, Admiral Kogo did not light up his customary Havana Perfecto.

Instead, he sat politely at the polished mahogany conference table and doodled on his yellow note pad.

His peers, splendid in dress white uniforms stiff with decorations and gold braid, sat politely, like a cage full of circus tigers; each tiger sitting on its tub, each tiger performing its predictable routine, each tiger waiting for a mistake to happen.

"Rosinante has honored their agreement," said Shinaka. "We have received their technical data for building the heat ray. Please consider: should we now enter into a mutual defense pact with them as we suggested we might do?"

"We have extended diplomatic recognition," said Admiral Takoba. "Surely that is sufficient?"

"That was necessary," said Admiral Kogo, "assuming, of course, that we did not wish to reinvent the heat ray ourselves. A mutual defense pact ought to be approved on its own merits."

"What are these merits, please?" asked Takoba.

"We are engaged in commerce raiding against the

North American Union base at Ceres," said Kogo. "Eventually we hope to take it over. Rosinante is now and will be close enough to sustain a supporting operation until the end of 2044. That is, the NAU can use Rosinante as a base to support Ceres until the NAU base orbiting Ceres grows too strong to strangle. With a mutual defense pact, we can deny the NAU the use of Rosinante, and the base at Ceres will fall like ripe fruit."

"There are other bases available to the NAU for this purpose, are there not?" asked Takoba politely.

"Obviously," replied Kogo. "But using them will cost more in time and treasure. When the will is weak, such difficulties may seem insurmountable."

"The NAU *has* been preoccupied with its civil war," Takoba agreed.

"Excuse me," said Admiral Konowaji, "but I think it is a mistake to enter into such an agreement with Rosinante. The hostility between Rosinante and the North American Union Government appears to be deep and bitter. Rosinante will hardly permit the NAU Navy to base a squadron there in the near future. Afterward, when the question of Ceres is settled, we will still have the treaty which you propose. I respectfully suggest that no treaty be signed."

"Excuse me, Grand Admiral," said Takoba, "but do I understand that you are in favor of such a treaty?"

"I have no opinion, Admiral Takoba," said Shinaka, returning Takoba's bow with a slight inclination of the head. "I seek consensus on the matter."

"I agree with Konowaji," said Takoba. "We do not need Rosinante."

A murmur of assent ran around the table.

"Admiral Kogo?" asked the Grand Admiral.

"We could use Rosinante's support," said Kogo blandly, "but I suspect it is not critically important."

"Do we need a mutual defense pact with them?" asked Shinaka.

"Need? I would say no," said Kogo politely.

"Then we will not propose such a pact," said Shinaka.

After the meeting, Grand Admiral Shinaka invited Admiral Kogo to the Flag Officers' Sushi Bar, an unauthorized extension of the Officers' Club in the basement. Shinaka had octopus, delicious thin slices of raw tentacle, and Kogo had raw tuna, splendidly fresh.

"This heat ray," said Shinaka, gesturing with his chopsticks, "it is a most troublesome thing. Why couldn't we have invented it ourselves so we could have suppressed it?"

A pretty kimono-clad waitress refilled their cups with green tea.

"It is implicit in the design of the Dragon Scale Mirror," said Kogo. "I expect the reason we didn't invent it was because we consciously decided not to." He ate a piece of tuna.

"I was with the Dragon Scale Mirror project as a senior team manager back in '23 when it was getting started," Kogo went on, "and the feature that most troubled the Admiralty at that time was the capability to use the mirror array as a defense against docking ships."

"A short-range defense only," said Shinaka. "Why were they troubled?"

"A city wall is a short-range defense," replied Kogo, wishing he could light up a cigar, "but when a city builds such a wall it may suddenly become more adventuresome in its foreign policy. The Admiralty feared the drift away from the Central Government. The habitats lend themselves to autarky very naturally. If they also become defensible, like castles, how will we be able to collect our taxes? The big laser was considered in that context, and we never went ahead with it because the Admiralty was afraid that such a powerful weapon in the hands of the habitat managers would make them impossible to control. That is what bothers you now, isn't it?"

"Yes," said Shinaka, eating a piece of octopus. "It

diminishes our warships, also. Perhaps that bothers me even more."

"I can see your point," said Kogo, removing a cigar from his pocket.

"Do not smoke, please," said the Grand Admiral, taking a disk of seaweed-wrapped rice. Kogo shrugged and put away his Havana Perfecto.

"It does not matter," said Kogo, "the heat ray is there. Either we use it to advantage or we do not, but we cannot make it disappear. Consider that to use it one must have the Dragon Scale Mirror—which is standard on Japanese habitats, while only a small number of non-Japanese habitats have them. If we use it, we will have a significant military advantage for a significant length of time." He smiled, showing his lower teeth. "I say build it!"

The waitress brought Shinaka another order of octopus.

"It is true," conceded Shinaka, taking a fresh slice, "we would achieve a transient advantage with the device. What did you have in mind?"

"Use it to free our Navy from defending fixed and scattered points," said Kogo, "so that we can concentrate our forces for a decisive victory!"

"The last time we did that was when we developed the Zero fighter plane at the beginning of World War II," said Shinaka. "What happens afterward?"

"The secret of the heat ray is out, Grand Admiral," said Kogo, taking a sip of tea. "Whatever will happen afterward can no longer be prevented. The only question is: will we step through this tiny window of opportunity that has opened for us?"

"Let us analyze the device from Rosinante first," said Shinaka. "It may be we can improve it, or it may be useless. It is madness to ride off to war with a bamboo spear."

Mexico, torn from the North American Union, split along a line running from Mazatlán to Torreón to Monterrey to the Rio Grande west of Brownsville.

To the south, General Pablo Cuevas led the junta that ruled the Democratic Republic of Mexico from Mexico City.

To the north, General Vincente Martin Morales proclaimed himself President of the United States of Mexico, and Dallas his seat of government.

By and large, the L-4 Fleet followed Admiral Antonio Jimenez and rallied to Morales and the USM.

There were, of course, exceptions.

The battleship *Wyoming* and three or four cruisers remained loyal to the ideal of restoring the Old Regime. It was not accidental that on these ships the Hispanic officers and rating had transferred out.

Neither was it accidental that the Anglo officers and ratings that stayed tended to be Old Regimists. Given the mobility of personnel in the fleet, it was inevitable that such a selection should have taken place.

Admiral Jimenez needed experienced hands. The USM, despite Hulvey's policy of population exchange, retained a large Anglo minority. Many, convinced that the Old Regime was dead forever, joined Jimenez. Conversely, many also came the other way.

The Old Regimists sat with their tiny fleet in the big naval base at L-4 Lambda-1 and watched the world go by.

CHAPTER 19

On the morning of January 19, 2042, the Council of Rosinante met to consider the question of secession from the North American Union.

The principal opposition came from the minority

stockholder, Mason Fox, chief executive officer of G.Y. Fox, Inc.

"There has been a great deal of talk about 'freedom,' " said Fox, his shock of unruly red hair belying the formality of his dark blue suit, "but it is hard to imagine how Rosinante could be more free. What taxes have you paid to the NAU? None!"

"We have an enormous deduction in the form of our debt service," said Cantrell, "but ask also, what benefits have we received. *Also* none. Right? Of course right!"

"Stop interrupting me, Charlie," Fox said. "I want to know why you are all so hell-bent on taking this—this leap in the dark. Nobody answers me."

"Hey, Mason," said Cantrell, "when I saw Bunjiro off at the elevator, the Rosinante Militia passed in review with the flag cased—they had the North American Union flag *cased*! I tried to find out who had ordered it done, and every officer in the battalion accepted responsibility. They flew the Stars and Stripes too—and I was afraid to ask about *it* because what if they told me the same thing? Do you know what the band played? 'Tomorrow Belongs to Me.' "

"That's been in the band's repertoire for quite a while, Charles," said Marian.

"But I never knew the words!" Cantrell said. "They had a high tenor singing them, and the battalion was the chorus: 'Oh, Fatherland, Fatherland show us the sign that your children have waited to see! The morning will come when this world is mine, tomorrow belongs to me!' The Militia wants independence. Mason, you tell me what the advantages of staying with the North American Union are!"

"They'll build a Navy base here," said Fox.

"Sure they will," agreed Cantrell, "and that will be just fine for your ship-repair business, won't it?"

"I don't deny it," said Fox, "but it will be good for the whole community as well."

"Nobody asked you to come to Rosinante, Mr. Fox,"

said Big John Bogdanovitch. "Why did you come? If you don't like it here, why don't you leave?"

"I came because the Mexicans were taking over the L-4s," said Fox. "If I was lucky, they might have paid off my business five cents on the dollar. More likely I'd have got a big fat nothing. I'm not leaving because right now I haven't got a pot to piss in! There is no place to go. None."

"You are a wealthy man, Mr. Fox," said Bogdanovitch. "Surely you could go anywhere you wanted. The L-5s, or Laputa, or LaCanaria, even. You could go back to Tellus if you wanted. Why stay here?"

"Because my business is here. I've set up my business here. Without it, I'm nothing. A coupon-clipper, no richer than a retired civil servant, talking about what I used to do when I ran my own business."

"I see," said Bogdanovitch, folding his huge hands on the table before him. "So Rosinante is to do what is good for *your* business?"

"He is the chief minority stockholder in Rosinante, Inc.," said Corporate Forziati. "We owe him the courtesy of a hearing before we decide."

"Certainly Mr. Fox won't find any cheaper rent," said Corporate Susan. "I can see why he'd like the Navy to do business *here*."

"That's beside the point!" said Fox. "Charlie says he's going along with this reckless drift to independence because the militia wants it. Right, Charlie?"

"That's one reason, Mason."

"I thought you were the *boss,* Charlie—I thought what you said *went*—I thought you were the goddamned *Governor* of this place!"

"I am, Mason," said Cantrell, "and I need the militia to stay that way. Rosinante is all I have. Without it I've got the rug on my office floor. I am very sorry your business may suffer, but I will not risk losing Rosinante."

"You're risking it by splitting with the NAU," said Fox. "For God's sake, Charlie, if you want to play it safe, send Captain Lovell back to Laputa and stay in the NAU!"

"No," said Cantrell.

"That's Lowell," said Marian.

"Why not?" Fox was not angry, only baffled.

"We've been over this ground before," said Cantrell. "Captain Lowell is my guest. That is sufficient."

"I don't understand what's going on," said Mason Fox.

The initial vote for independence was 5–0, with Corporate Forziati abstaining.

"You can't abstain," said Fox. "I demand that you vote, and I demand that you vote NO!"

"May I reconsider my abstention, Mr. Chairman?" asked Corporate Forziati.

"You may," said Cantrell.

"It is my belief that independence will prove beneficial to all the stockholders of Rosinante, Inc., minority as well as majority. I do not agree with Mr. Fox's arguments, nor with his analysis. I cast my vote for independence."

"Well, I'll be damned!" said Mason Fox.

"That makes it unanimous," said Charles Cantrell.

Marian Yashon walked into Cantrell's office and handed him a piece of hard copy.

"Look at that," she said. "Take a *good* look at it."

Cantrell took the paper and put on his glasses.

The letterhead was the Stars and Stripes of the United States of America, in full color, flanked by an armored marine holding a Stangl rifle over his head, and a somewhat generalized computer drawing of a cruiser. Underneath it said: THE OLD REGIMIST SQUADRON (ORS) L-4 FLEET.

23 January '42

Dear Governor Cantrell:

The 85th Caucus of ORS Senior Officers has unanimously voted to congratulate Rosinante on the decision to become independent of the North American Union.

We also wish to express our profound satisfaction at the support that you have given to Captain Robert Lowell, a brother officer and comrade-in-arms.

SS *Wyoming*
> Captain Simon R. Whelan
> First Officer Nathan McClusky
> Executive Officer C.W. Tower
> CPO Jane Lane, Chair, Ratings Council

SS *Havana*
> Commander L. Burton Halliday, Administrator
> Captain Louis J. Carr III, Union President

SS *Halifax*
> Captain Stephen C.T. Rice
> Lieutenant Commander Elizabeth Blanchard, Ship's Surgeon
> Lieutenant Commander Paul Casey, Union Steward

SS *San Francisco*
> W.W. Johnstone, Acting Captain

SS *Tampa*
> CPO Gloria diLido

"I thought we'd just picked Lowell as the issue to fight over because we didn't want to try to explain about Corporate Susan," said Cantrell.

"So we did," said Marian. She drew herself a cup of coffee and sat down alongside his desk. "But these people think it's great. Look at the list of signatures, Charles."

"I don't know any of these people," he said. "What about them?"

"Look at the titles," said Marian. "Don't they talk to you?"

"Frankly, no," said Cantrell. "If they talk to you, what do they say?"

"They say chaos," she replied, taking a sip of her coffee. "Look at the *Wyoming*—a 'first officer' and an 'executive officer' without any rank indicated. I'll bet Whelan isn't a real captain, either. And on the *Havana*, we have an 'administrator,' for God's sake, and a captain who is also either *a* Union president or maybe *the* Union President. You don't have the same pattern of officers on any two ships. No overall command structure. Going on a year after the revolution, and they still aren't organized!"

"It's only a little over half a year," said Cantrell.

"No Hispanic surnames, either," said Marian. "I expect they migrated out of the ORS to join Admiral Jimenez. Think about it, Charles—what sort of people are left there?"

"Old Regimists," said Cantrell, after a moment.

He walked over and closed the blinds a little against the bright morning sunlight pouring into his office.

"Die-hard Old Regimists. Radical Anglos. Known traitors who can't go back no matter what happens. Professional WASPs, like some of the Alamo students we have here."

"All of those," said Marian, setting her coffee cup on Cantrell's desk, "but they are also Navy people—chaos isn't natural for them. They don't like it, but they don't know what to do about it.

"You have an opportunity, Charles."

"You mean invite them to Rosinante?" he said. "Suppose they came? What would we do with them?"

"Having a fleet—even a little fleet—might encourage the Japanese to sign a mutual defense pact, for one thing," she said. "It would also do a lot to discourage the NAU Navy from coming after us."

"Isn't that what the Purple Shaft is for?" asked Cantrell.

"Yes. Will we be better or worse off if we have a Navy?"

"Would the ships make a difference, Tiger?"

Marian took a sip of her coffee. "The ships would make a difference, Charles. I can't see the NAU Navy sending a fleet that could deal with a battleship, four cruisers, *and* the big laser. The Japanese call it a heat ray, incidentally, which isn't a bad name. Lasers have no glamor, no pizzazz. The point is, though, that by coming here the ORS can segue from revolution to secession. I think they'd settle down, and I think the ships would be a plus for our side."

"You don't think they'd get together with that asshole Guthrie Moore and his revolutionary turkey party?"

"Why should Moore get any respect from them?" she said.

"Okay, Tiger, we invite them." Cantrell stood up, and began walking around the room. "Why should they come?"

"In the first place, you aren't inviting them," Marian paused to take a sip of coffee. "You are offering to accept their allegiance. You are saying: I can use your service if you are willing to serve. You are a chance to climb out of chaos back to being a real Navy again. They will never get a better offer."

"I can see that," said Cantrell. "It might be nice for the Old Regimists to take the waters at Rosinante. But is there any compelling reason why they should come?"

Marian finished her coffee and set the cup on his desk.

"Figure it out—the ORS is between the Mexican Navy and the NAU Navy, and it doesn't belong to either one. They can't stay where they are. When the L-5 Fleet gets refitted and overhauled, I would expect it will move over to the L-4s and clean up the ORS as its first order of business."

"A naval action?" asked Cantrell, turning to face her.

"Probably not," said Marian. "The threat of a naval action ought to be sufficient to disperse the ORS. A little elementary diplomacy."

Cantrell opened his blue desk dictionary and leafed through it.

"My dictionary defines diplomacy as 'conducting relations between nations, as in making agreements,' " said Cantrell. "The threat of naval action is diplomacy?"

"Oh hell yes, Charles. What do you think diplomacy is, anyway?" Marian sat back and crossed her arms. "The use of force between nations is war, the threat to use force is diplomacy. Sweet reason is for explaining what happened afterward."

"Come on, Tiger, diplomacy is negotiating mutually beneficial agreements."

"How do you think nations agree on who gets the lion's share of those mutual benefits, Charles?" she asked. "Force is there, always. If it isn't used, it's because the diplomats on both sides are in agreement on the way it balances out. Just because a threat is implicit doesn't mean it isn't a threat."

"Okay, Tiger. Let's say I make the ORS an offer. Is that diplomacy?"

Marian thought for a second. "Yes," she said.

"Fine. Where is the threat to use force?"

Marian studied her empty coffee cup. "You aren't dealing one on one, Charles. The direct threat to the ORS is coming from the L-5 Fleet, an arm of the NAU. The ORS is engaged in a civil war with the NAU, otherwise you wouldn't have any leverage. If they come to Rosinante, they eliminate the threat of being wiped out by the L-5 Fleet, and effectively withdraw from their civil war."

"Right. I agree, Tiger." Cantrell removed his glasses and put them back in their case. "But where did *I* threaten to use force?"

"You didn't threaten, Charles, you promised," she said. "If the NAU comes out here after them—contrary to what I believe will happen—you have promised to use Rosinante's force on their behalf."

Cantrell walked over to the coffee urn and drew himself a cup of coffee. "Would you like another cup?" he asked.

"No, thank you," she said.

"That could be risky," he said at last. "Of course we're in deep trouble already. As far as I can see, any downside from having the ORS out here is in the medium to long term. The upside is immediate. You think we ought to invite them out to tea?"

"I think so," said Marian. "I'll draft a letter for you to send off. Will you want Council approval?"

"Yes," said Cantrell. He summoned Skaskash and Susan Brown.

The two computers split the telecon screen, Corporate Susan appearing in her white lab coat, Skaskash appearing as Toshiro Mifune playing an itinerant samurai.

"Hai?!" said Skaskash.

"Read this," said Marian, placing the ORS letter face down on the telecon platen.

"Ah, so," said Skaskash. "Very interesting. Do you plan to invite them to come here?"

"I shall bring the matter to the Council's attention," said Cantrell. "Perhaps we will. But I would like your opinion on the matter."

"Mrrrmnh!" said the voice of Mifune.

"You are looking for possible allies in our war with the NAU?" asked Corporate Susan.

"I would say we may be looking *at* possible allies," said Marian. "What do you think?"

"It depends," said Corporate Susan "Who do you have in mind to be Fleet Admiral if and when they come?"

"I hadn't thought about it," said Cantrell. "Captain Lowell, maybe?"

"No!" said Corporate Susan, Skaskash, and Marian in unison.

"He can be on the Admiral's staff," said Marian, "but he has managed to lose his ship twice in less than a year. I don't want him as Admiral."

"His loyalty to Rosinante is questionable," said Skaskash. "We have done him a great service, and he may be so overwhelmed with gratitude that he will come to resent us."

"I don't know him," said Corporate Susan. "Surely there is local talent that can command a small fleet?"

"Shall I take the position, then?" asked Cantrell.

"No," said Marian. "You couldn't do justice to the job of Commander in Chief if you also wore the Admiral's hat."

"I'm open to suggestion," said Cantrell. "Who do you have in mind?"

"Corporate Susan Brown," said Skaskash. "It will take fifty to sixty days for the ORS to get here, depending on how soon they leave. That will provide ample time to master the strategy involved." On the telecon screen Mifune eased the hilt of his sword clear of the scabbard a few inches, then returned it with a decisive gesture. "Most of the problems are trivial," it added, "mere exercises in logistics and supply."

"Are you willing to be the Admiral of the Old Regimist Squadron?" Marian asked.

"Yes," said Corporate Susan, "although it will have to be renamed. The Rosinante High Space Fleet, perhaps."

"Very good," said Marian. "Shall I prepare a reply for the ORS to that effect and present it to the full Council for approval—say at 1500 hours this afternoon?"

"Hai!" said Skaskash with a formal bow.

"Of course," said Corporate Susan.

Cantrell took a sip of coffee.

"I guess that's the way to go," he said at last.

CHAPTER 20

On the morning of February 1, 2042, President Oysterman had a working breakfast in the little dining room
overlooking the atrium of the Executive Mansion in St.
Louis. The Administrators of his various agencies were
served orange juice, scrambled or fried eggs, link sausage, home fries, toast and jelly, and coffee, or, in the
case of William Hulvey, tea. In the Old Regime it
would have been called a Cabinet meeting.

"The resettlement program in Southern California,"
said the President, "is that going well, do you think?"

"We have about a quarter million Texicans still in
tents," said Branigan, Administrator of Housing and
Urban Management, "but we've cleared away about
twenty-five square kilometers of the burnt-out barrio in
Los Angeles, and we ought to be letting the first building contracts sometime this week."

"That's splendid," said the President. "What do you
think of that, Mr. Hulvey?"

"Just fine, sir," Hulvey said. "I have tried to expe-
dite matters by passing the word along—unofficially, of
course—to the contractors."

"What did you tell them?" asked Branigan.

"Steal in moderation," said Hulvey. "No damn reason they can't do good work fast and still make
money."

The President tittered. "Steal in moderation," he
said. "Oh, that's rich, Mr. Hulvey."

Hulvey's belt phone rang.

"Admiral Vong here," said a familiar voice. "You asked to be informed immediately if the Old Regimists made any move. Can you talk?"

"I'm at breakfast with the President," Hulvey said, "but tell me what happened anyway."

"The ORS moved out of the Lambda-1 base about an hour ago," said Vong.

"Which ships?"

"The SS *Wyoming*, the heavy cruiser *San Francisco*, and the scout cruisers *Halifax, Havana,* and *Tampa.* They have been joined by two, possibly three merchant ships."

"What happened?" asked the President.

"The ORS—the Old Regimist Squadron—just pulled out of Lambda-1," said Hulvey. "Maybe an hour ago."

"Is that Admiral Vong calling?" asked the President. "Why don't you put him on the telecon, and we can all hear this exciting news?"

"I'm going to transfer you to a telecon," said Hulvey. "Don't get lost in there, Admiral."

"Good enough," said Vong's voice from an unlit telecon set. "Please wait until I can get into a telecon seat."

"What do you propose to do about this Old Regimist Squadron?" asked Gradier, Administrator of Agriculture.

"Destroy them," said Hulvey.

"I thought the question was addressed to me," complained the President.

"I beg your pardon, Mr. President," said Hulvey, "I must have been carried away by the excitement of the moment."

Vong appeared on the telecon screen, quite splendid in his dress blues, which were generated, press and all, by the Admiral's personal computer.

"I believe you know everybody here, Admiral Vong," said Hulvey. "You had a question, Mr. President?"

"Why yes, I believe I did, Mr. Hulvey. —Ah, Admiral Vong, these ships of yours, where are they headed?"

"Out," said Vong. "In a few days we'll have a fix on

their course, but I expect they are en route to Rosinante."

"In the asteroids?" asked the President.

"Yes, sir."

"Well, good riddance to them," said the President. "Maybe now we can get back to putting the country together again without those awful people trying to restore the Old Regime." He took a sip of his orange juice. "Mr. Hulvey, why do you want to destroy that little band of silly men? Why don't you just let them go?"

"Because they deny the legitimacy of our regime," said Hulvey, "they are a threat to the life."

"Oh, tush, Mr. Hulvey. The rest of the L-4 Fleet is much bigger, and *it* isn't a threat, is it?"

"The rest of the L-4 Fleet joined the United States of Mexico—a state that we have recognized and which recognizes us. It may be a threat—any fleet may be a threat—but it is not seeking our overthrow, and we are not at war."

"That's really very encouraging, Mr. Hulvey," said the President. "Admiral Vong, do you really think the ships are going to Rosinante?"

"Yes, Mr. President. The last two days, the ORS Caucus has been talking about nothing else."

"ORS Caucus?" asked the President.

"The Old Regimist Squadron Caucus of Senior Officers," said Vong. "You might call it the nearest thing to a government the mutineers have."

"I see, I see," said the President. "And Rosinante, under this fellow Cantrell, didn't they say they were part of Texas? Yes . . . they said they were part of Texas and seceded from the NAU a few days ago." The President tittered. "A part of Texas out in the asteroids, that's hilarious."

"Yes, Mr. President," said Branigan, smiling a *pro forma* smile.

"Are they—Rosinante—trying to overthrow our regime, Mr. Hulvey?" asked the President.

"They are known to be sympathetic to the Old Regime," replied Hulvey.

"Do you take me for a simpleton, Mr. Hulvey?!" shouted President Oysterman, clenching his small hands into fists. "I demand you answer my question!"

"Then I must say probably not, Mr. President," Hulvey said. "Governor Cantrell expressed the hope that we might live in peace together, as you probably remember."

"I *do* remember," said the President. "How terribly clever of you to know what I'm remembering." He turned to the Administrator of NAUGA-State. "Mr. Adams, sir. Why can't we recognize Rosinante like we do the two Mexicos?"

"Why, ah, why, ah, why I don't know why, ah, we can't," said Adams. "We, ah, are about to recognize Cuba, ah, after all."

"Oh splendid," said the President. "If we recognize Rosinante, and this—this ORS Caucus, did you call it?—goes there, then Governor Cantrell will make them behave, won't he? What do you think, Admiral Vong?"

Vong looked at Hulvey, and then back to the President. "Yes, Mr. President, I believe Cantrell would take care of them." His eyes flicked back to Hulvey for a moment. "Even if you wished to pursue them, the ORS, Caucus and all, would be halfway to Rosinante before we could send the Fleet out after them."

Vong looked squarely at Hulvey. "There are a number of scout cruisers that could depart sooner, but it seems poor tactics to send out the fleet piecemeal."

"I am so glad you agree with me, Admiral," said the President. "You don't agree with me, do you, Mr. Hulvey? I can tell by the way you hunch your shoulders, but that is just, as you like to say, too fucking bad!" the President tittered.

"That takes care of two birds with one stone, and think of the money we'll save! Why, we could use it to rebuild the Los Angeles barrio, couldn't we, Mr. Branigan?"

"We could indeed," agreed Branigan heartily. "Yes, sir, Mr. President, that is one place we could really use the money!"

"Oh, bully," said the President, grinning. "And what do you think of my policy, Mr. Hulvey?"

"I don't like it." Hulvey speared the last cold link sausage on his plate and ate it.

"I can't deny that it may be good for the country, though," he added.

"Oh, Mr. Hulvey," said the President, "I do so admire your evenhanded fairness! It takes a really big man to admit that a 'pitiful wimp' may be right and he is wrong, *doesn't* it, Mr. Hulvey?"

"What's next on your agenda, Admiral Vong?" said Branigan hastily.

"We are preparing to send a task force to support our bases around Ceres. As you know, we have been having trouble with Japanese commerce raiders."

Governor Charles Cantrell called the Council of Rosinante into special session at 2300 hours on February 9, 2042.

"I trust you have all had an opportunity to study the proposition put forth by NAUGA-State," he said. "I solicit your comments."

"It is very strange that this should be coming from NAUGA-State, rather than NAUGA-Navy," said Bogdanovitch.

"Face it, Big John," said Dornbrock, "this cockamamie idea would look strange no matter *who* put it out. Oysterman is trying to save money by contracting out the NAU's naval operations, for God's sake!"

"Dornbrock has hit it," said Marian. "The NAU is offering us a fortune to use a squadron of ships we don't even have yet. But they offer only diplomatic recognition, not a mutual defense pact. Only money, not weapons."

"Money *is* a weapon," said Corporate Forziati, mildly.

"Damn it, Forziati, Oysterman is trying to hire us as mercenaries!" said Marian.

"Following Machiavelli's usage, I would say 'auxiliaries' instead," said Skaskash. "Mercenaries are hired on an individual basis by their captain, who is in turn hired on a piecework basis, so to speak. Auxiliaries are in the full-time employ of their prince, who leases them out. The ORS clearly falls in the latter category. We have already voted the individual members of the squadron citizenship in Rosinante."

"Dr. Yashon has a point," said Corporate Susan. "Accept the NAU's offer, and we become involved with defending the NAU's bases around Ceres. Against whom? Against Japan. If Japan chooses to wage war against Rosinante, who will come to our aid? Nobody. Who could we turn to? Nobody. Who would mourn our demise? A few people on Ceres. What is the downside? Total destruction!"

"The upside is that the NAU is offering a *lot* of money," said Corporate Forziati, "and what will you do with the ORS if you don't accept the NAU's offer? Teach them to farm?"

"Mason Fox would really like to skim some of that money off, wouldn't he now?" asked Corporate Susan.

"Wouldn't we all?" asked Corporate Forziati. "If there were no element of risk, would the rewards be so great?"

"There is also a risk in not accepting the offer," said Cantrell. "If NAUGA-Navy is, or was, preparing a relief expedition to Ceres, the most logical base for them to operate from is right here. Either they will make us an offer we can't refuse, or the Japanese will. We will be a tiny nation trying to stay neutral in a strategic spot in a big war."

"So let the NAU Navy come out here and *then* choose sides," said Marian. "Just because you don't catch the first opportunity to plunge into a war doesn't mean there'll never be another!"

"Will you yourself decide your fate, or will you drift willy-nilly on the rushing stream of events, to wherever the current takes you?" said Bogdanovitch.

"That's very pretty, Big John," said Marian. "Does it mean you think we ought to do it?"

"Well, yes, actually," said Bogdanovitch. "I myself

have always felt a patriotic attachment to the North American Union, and it seems proper to come to her aid in time of trouble."

"We are citizens of Rosinante," said Corporate Susan. "Not the NAU. Vote for your best interests, not your sloppy sentimentality."

"We were citizens of the NAU long before there was such a place as Rosinante," said Bogdanovitch. "We have old loyalties and roots we cannot dismiss lightly."

"We are going to temporize in this business," said Cantrell. "We will say yes, this looks very nice, but we want a mutual defense treaty, and maybe more money as well. Nevertheless, I wish to poll the Council on their feelings about it. Marian?"

"I am bitterly opposed," she said. "If there is any way to avoid accepting this offer, we should so avoid it."

"Skaskash?"

"I agree with Marian," said the computer. "Unfortunately, I believe that we will be unable to avoid accepting the offer."

"Big John?"

"Get more money if you can, but go with the NAU," said Bogdanovitch.

"Don?"

"It's a good offer. I'd say go with it as it stands and put some people back to work," said Dornbrock. "We'd have some real work for the first time in years."

"Forziati?"

"I say take it," said Corporate Forziati, "but it won't hurt to ask for more."

"Dr. Brown?"

"As you know, most of the Alamo corvée favors a fight. I don't think they care whether they fight the NAU or Japan. But you might be surprised to learn that the vast majority of the Korean-Japanese women are against any accommodation with Japan whatsoever," said Corporate Susan. "Also, I find the course of naval studies I have undertaken to be utterly fascinating. I can see how such an interest would become compulsive for a human. I would enjoy being a wartime admiral, I really would. However, none of this offsets the fact that contracting to fight the NAU's war with Japan is a monumentally dumb move.

"I do not approve," said Corporate Susan Brown. "In the end we may have no choice, but I do not approve."

"I see," said Cantrell. "Skaskash, would you draft a letter asking for a mutual defense treaty and about one and a half times what they offered?"

Skaskash faded from the telecon screen to be replaced by the letter.

The Council read it in silence.

"What happens when President Oysterman comes back and says fine?" asked Marian. "The treaty has to be ratified by the Senate, you know."

"Then we go with it," said Cantrell. "If the Senate doesn't ratify the treaty, that gives us a chance to cancel out."

"No, Charles," said Marian, "the NAU Senate can debate and delay and mess around with the treaty while we bleed to death. We'll never be able to cancel, not while there's fighting to do."

"I expect you're right," said Cantrell. "Make that twice what they offered, Skaskash."

CHAPTER 21

Power is an illusion, maintained by persuading people that you are powerful. Mirrors help, but self-delusion helps even more. Self-delusion fed by the desire to wield power.

OFFICE OF THE ADMINISTRATOR
NAUGA-Army, -Navy, -Security

14 February '42

Dear Mr. President:

Our disagreement in the matter of contracting out the defense of Ceres has become too broad and too deep for any accommodation.

Please accept my resignation as the Administrator of NAUGA-Army, -Navy, and -Security, effective immediately.

If you wish, I will continue in an acting capacity until the Senate ratifies your selections for my replacements, but I feel this would be unwise.

Sincerely,

/s/

William Marvin Hulvey

THE EXECUTIVE MANSION

14 February '42

Dear Mr. Hulvey:

It is with deep regret that I accept your resignation.

Your strong leadership has been invaluable in the

past, and the historians of the future may well acclaim you as the architect of the new North American Union.

Please clean out your several desks by close-of-business today.

Sincerely,

/s/

Dr. Henry Oysterman, President

The resignation of the Triple Administrator remained an insoluble puzzle to the pundits and powers of official St. Louis. By all rights he should have forced Oysterman to resign, or, more simply, he should have killed him, and then seized the reins of power in his own capable hands.

Eventually, they decided that Hulvey resigned out of his devotion to the NAU, that by resigning he had insured its survival. They could not imagine a man in position to seize power who did not do so because he did not want power any longer.

CHAPTER 22

The 1,342 officers and ratings of the Old Regimist Squadron formed up in front of the Japanese Pavilion with their dependents. Behind them the band played softly.

At precisely 0800 the *shoji* screens slid back and Governor Cantrell walked to the podium.

"Good morning, ladies and gentlemen," he said. "Some of you may know me from my pictures, some of you have met with me personally. I am Charles Chavez Cantrell, Governor of Rosinante, and we are gathered here together so that you may take the oath of citizenship, the formal acceptance of Rosinante as your new fatherland.

"Raise your right hand and repeat after me: I, say your own name"—the crowd raised their right hands and began to repeat the oath—"on this day, April 23, 2042, hereby declare, on oath, that I absolutely and entirely renounce and abjure all allegiance and fidelity to any state or sovereignty to which I have heretofore been a subject or citizen, or would have been a subject or citizen if such a state or sovereignty had in fact existed. From this time forth I will support and defend the State of Rosinante as that state may lawfully require. I take this obligation freely without any mental reservation, so help me God.

"You are now citizens of Rosinante. You also constitute the Navy of Rosinante, and I now call upon you, those of you who are able and willing, to signify your enlistment in the Navy of Rosinante by taking a single step forward."

The crowd took a single step forward, including several small children.

"Some of you are a little young, there, but welcome aboard anyway."

There was a ripple of laughter.

"Since you are now the Navy of Rosinante, it is fitting that your ships be rechristened," said Cantrell.

Behind him a movie screen was lowered, and simultaneously Skaskash slowly worked the mirrors to send the bright morning sun back below the horizon.

Cantrell walked the podium to the side of the stage.

The image of the *Halifax* appeared on the screen, with the image of Governor Cantrell standing on a platform that never was, waiting for his cue.

"Since we are a space-dwelling people," said Cantrell, live on stage, "it is redundant to refer to our ships as 'spaceships.' They are simply Rosinante Navy Ships, RNS.

"Since we are not a new people, our homelands have histories, and our ancestors a lineage as ancient and honorable as any in the Solar System. One day our children will surely ask who they are, and what burden of history they carry forward.

"Our people come from the North American Union, and disproportionately from Texas. They come from Japan, and disproportionately of Korean stock.

"Our history is rooted in the wars of Earth, of the distant planet we call Tellus, and this has shaped the design of our institutions and buildings as surely as it has left its imprint on our spirit.

"This scout cruiser I now rechristen RNS *Tet*," said Cantrell.

On the movie screen the image of Cantrell cut a ribbon, and a cargo net carrying a Nebuchadnezzar of champagne rode on a trolley line to smash against the armored stem of the cruiser. It made a barely visible spot of white foam.

"The name invokes a battle in the Vietnamese war, a battle where the armies of our ancestors, American and Korean, defeated the enemy on the ground, only to lose the hearts and minds of their own people. The name was chosen to remind us that it is necessary to fight smart as well as hard, to *know* that what we fight for is right, as well as fighting for what is right. To remind us that victory, like defeat, is an illusion that one conjures with mirrors."

The image of the RNS *Tet* dissolved, and was replaced by the cruiser *Havana*.

"This scout cruiser I now rechristen RNS *Pearl Harbor*," said Cantrell.

Again, the Cantrell on the screen cut the ribbon to make an insignificant spot of champagne on the stem of the cruiser.

"This name invokes the beginning of a great war between Japan and the United States of America." There was a cheer, which he allowed to die down. "We choose to remember it, as we are Japanese, as a brilliant tactical victory. We choose to remember it, as we are

Americans, as the defeat that inspired the enthusiasm of a mighty people. The name was chosen to remind us that in war the spiritual and moral values of a people are of paramount importance, and that war is the ultimate test of these values. Once again, we are reminded that victory and defeat are the images in the conjurer's mirror."

The image of the RNS Pearl Harbor dissolved and was replaced by the cruiser *Tampa*.

"This scout cruiser I now rechristen the RNS *Hampton Roads*," said Cantrell.

Again, the cut ribbon and the distant spot of champagne.

"This name invokes the War Between the States," said Cantrell. "Shiloh would have been lovelier, but Hampton Roads was the place where the *Monitor* fought the *Merrimac*. We remember it because both sides sought to apply new technology in real time on a real battlefield. The battle itself was a hard-fought draw, when one side needed a clear-cut win. Victory and defeat come in many guises."

The image of the RNS *Hampton Roads* dissolved and was replaced by the cruiser *San Francisco*.

"This heavy cruiser I now rechristen the RNS *Inchon Landing*," said Cantrell.

Champagne spattered in the distance.

"This name invokes the war between Korea and the United States of America." This time there was applause, but no cheering. "We choose to remember it as the most brilliant victory of one of the most brilliant generals in our history. It was the stroke that won the war. Unfortunately, this same general, filled with the euphoria of victory, was unable to avoid the expansion of the war, as North Korea's ally, China, intervened. We cannot afford to entertain illusions of either victory or defeat, nor can we afford to indulge ourselves in the luxury of euphoria or the hopeless passivity of despair."

The image of the RNS *Inchon Landing* dissolved to be replaced by the far larger image of the *Wyoming*.

"This battleship I now rechristen the RNS *Alamo*," said Cantrell.

The champagne swung and splattered for the last time.

"Whatever this name invokes to some of you, it should also remind you that I am a politician, and that a key part of my constituency was, once, Texican Anglos. The lessons to be drawn from the Alamo are not inconsistent with the lessons I sought to draw from the other ships, but there is one thing that I would add. Setting aside all illusions, the memory of valor is a prize to cherish.

"We are now entered into a war with Japan that we can have no hope of 'winning' in the ordinary sense. We have accepted a contract from the NAU that we shall try to fulfill, not because we thought it a good idea, but because we had no better alternative. What is Ceres that we should die for her? Nothing. What has Japan done to earn our enmity or the North American Union our love? Nothing and again nothing.

"We have, however, one advantage. We, alone, are fighting for survival. The other principals, the North American Union and Japan, are barely aware that they are engaged, and in this there is real hope.

"That is all the ships we have to do," said Governor Cantrell. "May we have the sun back, Skaskash?"

When the sun had returned to its proper place in the sky, and the movie screen had rolled itself up, the officers of the Rosinante Navy went up to the Japanese Pavilion to be sworn in as individuals by Governor Cantrell personally.

At 1530 hours Cantrell climbed the staircase leading from the Japanese Pavilion to his office. He drew himself a cup of coffee, settled himself in his big desk chair, and removed his shoes.

"The North American Union Ambassador is here to present his credentials," said the receptionist.

"*Today?*" asked Cantrell. "Well, send him in. Wait. Send him in when I have my shoes back on."

A tall man with grizzled dark hair and an austere, sad face entered the room.

"How do you do, Governor Cantrell," he said easily. "I am William Marvin Hulvey."

Cantrell stood up, so astonished that if Hulvey had offered his hand, he would have shaken it.

"*You* are the NAU Ambassador?" he exclaimed. "What happened to the Honorable N. Joseph Saviano?"

"He remains on board ship waiting word from me," said Hulvey. "He will present his credentials directly, I expect, although then again, maybe not."

"What do you want?" asked Cantrell.

"I'd like to congratulate you on your contract negotiations for the relief of Ceres," said Hulvey. "You made many of the points against the idea that I, also, had made. And expressed them with such undiplomatic candor and force, too."

"Why, thank you," said Cantrell. "It wasn't too different from labor negotiations, once we understood that we couldn't refuse. But you could have sent a letter for that. Why are you here?"

"To exchange information," replied Hulvey. "I wish to ask Corporate Dr. Susan Brown about the notebook of Dr. Heinrich von Zwang. In return, I will tell you what I know about Joe Bob Baroody and GNM 1848."

"Very well," said Cantrell, "may I bring in some of my people?"

"Be my guest," said Hulvey. "I, in turn, would like to bring in Corporate Elna."

"That will be no problem," said Cantrell. "We have a number of extra telecon screens available."

"I prefer that she not appear on a telecon screen," said Hulvey politely. "It bothers me to have my machine mimicking a human being. Corporate Elna is in the waiting room."

They took their places around the dark gray conference table that would no longer fit in the Council Chamber, the one with the gold inlay of the Rosinante Logo. Governor Cantrell and Marian Yashon at one end, flanked by Corporate Skaskash and Corporate Dr.

Susan Brown on separate telecon screens, faced William Hulvey at the other end, with the tall, massive bulk of Corporate Elna at his right hand.

"Shall we begin?" asked Cantrell.

"I suppose so," said Hulvey. "Dr. Brown, would you tell me what you know about the von Zwang notebook?"

"I studied it in great detail for the better part of two years," said Corporate Susan. "It is probable that I know a lot more about it than you would care to hear. Have you a more specific question?"

Hulvey looked at Corporate Elna and shrugged.

"Did von Zwang cross humans and chimpanzees?" asked Corporate Elna.

"No."

"Interesting, if true," said Corporate Elna. "Could you describe briefly what he did, then?"

"He claimed to have made such crosses," said Dr. Susan Brown. "My analysis of his work suggests very strongly that he was creating chimeras. He had a theory, as you may know, that the ova carried what he called 'genetic boilerplate,' standard, unchanging species-specific information. The chimeras he created were humans with a few *Pan trog.* genes grafted on, or vice versa. . . ."

"Pan trog?!" asked Cantrell.

"Short for *Pan troglodytes*—chimpanzees," said Dr. Susan Brown. "Just as *Homo sap.* is short for *Homo sapiens*—humans. Dr. von Zwang's theories were troublesome to us—to the genetic-research establishment— because they set forth the claim that human evolution was profoundly different. Potentially, they were the basis for a politically supported antievolutionist dogma that could never be refuted."

"I don't understand," said Cantrell. "What is a chimera, for instance?"

"A monster made up from pieces of different creatures," said Corporate Elna. "In this case, *Homo sap.* and *Pan trog.* Jennie Smith, the oldest of his creatures, was entirely human, with *Pan trog.* genes for autoimmune system, ductless glands, and liver grafted on to her genetic blueprint. Apparently, you couldn't tell her from a normal human, but she was, in fact, a chimera."

"Okay, I can see that," said Cantrell. "But why?"

"You could call it a religious dispute," said Dr. Susan Brown. "Von Zwang was lying through his teeth to support Hulvey's theology."

"I can see that, too," said Cantrell. "But why do you say the work could never be refuted?"

"Because no researcher would ever be willing to take the moral responsibility for creating a family—a race, even—of not-quite-human beings," said Dr. Susan Brown. Then she smiled. "At least no *human* researcher. That is the task *I* might have been created for. After we got von Zwang's notebook, the question became moot."

"How would von Zwang have disposed of the chimeras he created?" asked Marian.

"He never got that far," said Corporate Susan. "I have no idea."

"Interesting if true," said Marian. "I guess the question is really whether Mr. Hulvey here believes it. Do you, sir?"

"She's telling the truth," said Hulvey in a barely audible voice. A single tear formed in each eye and rolled slowly down his face.

"That was what von Zwang had agreed to do," said Corporate Elna. "The Creationist Coalition paid him to do it before we took power. To create a new theory as the basis for a Creationist dogma." The big machine paused. It might have been looking at its master. "After we had been supporting von Zwang's work for a few years, however, it became clear that we had no one in the movement who could evaluate it. A lot of us were not too happy with that state of affairs, and Stanley Bowman came up with an alternate plan. His idea was to expose von Zwang and denounce his evil experiments, and use guilt by association to smash the genetic-research establishment. In the event, the smashing of von Zwang's laboratory coincided with our taking power." Corporate Elna paused. "Perhaps it gave us the necessary impetus to take power—I don't know . . . One morning there was a rumor, and bang! The whole thing blew up."

"It's possible that the rumor which sent the Contra Darwin raiding party into von Zwang's lab was one that we'd started ourselves," said Hulvey, once more in control of himself. "I just didn't recognize it when it came back, is all."

He took a package of candy-coated chewing gum from his pocket, and slid the last piece into his hand.

"It could have been true," said Hulvey sadly. "I don't think I was wrong to believe the worst. And even then, if we had taken the notebook . . ." He shook his head. "Corporate Elna," he said, "I want you to cooperate with Governor Cantrell here as best as you ever can. You hear me?"

"Yes. I shall do so without reservation."

"Good." Hulvey put the candy-coated gum in his mouth and bit down on it.

"Good-bye, Willy," said Corporate Elna.

Hulvey turned toward the computer and toppled from his chair.

"Is he dead?" asked Marian, horrified.

"Yes, ma'am," replied the computer.

"I'll be in my office if you need me, Charles," Marian said. Cantrell nodded, and she left.

Cantrell looked from Hulvey's body on the floor to the dark, angular bulk of the computer. Somehow, the physical presence of the machine was disconcerting.

"Will you notify his next of kin?" he asked inanely. Hulvey's death would be front-page news over most of the Solar System.

"When I get plugged into the com-net," said the computer. Elna's voice, which had been female, now sounded curiously neuter.

"Ah, ahh . . . yeah. Sure," said Cantrell distractedly, staring at the body.

Eventually the ambulance that Skaskash had sent for arrived. Two men in pastel green coats walked in, lead-

ing a body cart. They loaded the corpse without ceremony and rolled it out, leaving behind a faint smell of
death.

"Take over, Skaskash," said Cantrell. At the door-
way he paused for a moment.

"I'll see you later, Elna," he said.

"Call me Corporate Hulvey," said the computer.